W9-BZD-247

the CRITTER club

#1
Amy and the Missing Puppy

#2
All About Ellie

#3
Liz Learns a Lesson

#4
Marion Takes a Break

by Callie Barkley ♥ illustrated by Marsha Riti

LITTLE SIMON

New York   London   Toronto   Sydney   New Delhi

LITTLE SIMON

An imprint of Simon & Schuster Children's Publishing Division • 1230 Avenue of the Americas, New York, New York 10020 • *Amy and the Missing Puppy, All About Ellie, Liz Learns a Lesson,* and *Marion Takes a Break* copyright © 2013 by Simon & Schuster, Inc. This Little Simon bind-up edition June 2015. All rights reserved, including the right of reproduction in whole or in part in any form. LITTLE SIMON is a registered trademark of Simon & Schuster, Inc., and associated colophon is a trademark of Simon & Schuster, Inc. For information about special discounts for bulk purchases, please contact Simon & Schuster Special Sales at 1-866-506-1949 or business@simonandschuster.com. The Simon & Schuster Speakers Bureau can bring authors to your live event. For more information or to book an event contact the Simon & Schuster Speakers Bureau at 1-866-248-3049 or visit our website at www.simonspeakers.com. Designed by Laura Roode

Manufactured in the United States of America 0118 FFG

10 9 8 7 6 5 4 3

ISBN 978-1-4814-5191-8

These titles were previously published individually by Little Simon.

Table of Contents

#1

Amy and the
Missing Puppy

• • • 5 • • •

#2

All About Ellie

• • • 127 • • •

#3

Liz Learns a Lesson

• • • 245 • • •

#4

Marion Takes a Break

• • • 363 • • •

the CRitteR club

Amy and the Missing Puppy

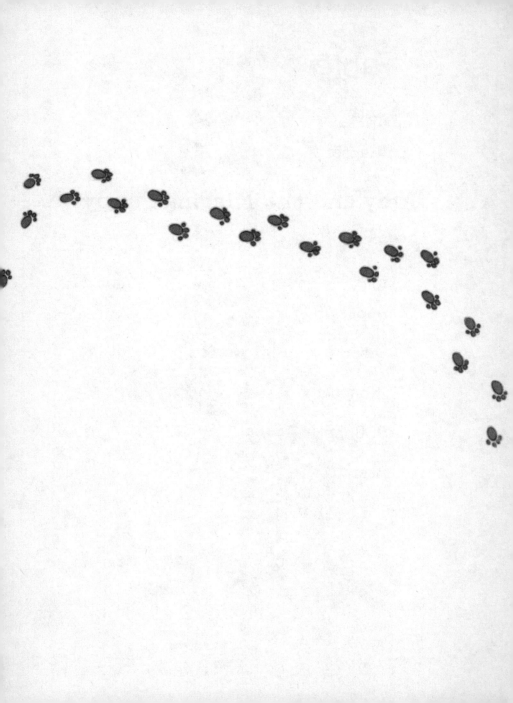

Table of Contents

Chapter 1   Spring Break Blues   9

Chapter 2   A New Friend   21

Chapter 3   Taking Out the Trash   35

Chapter 4   A Surprise Guest   43

Chapter 5   The First Clue!   53

Chapter 6   Rufus Was Here   59

Chapter 7   Follow That Puppy!   71

Chapter 8   A New Lead   85

Chapter 9   Gotcha!   99

Chapter 10   Ms. Sullivan's Idea   107

Chapter 11   The End and the Beginning   117

Spring Break Blues

Amy felt herself starting to blush. Her cheeks felt warm, then hot. Amy shook her short, light brown hair over her freckled face. She hoped it would hide her bright pink cheeks. *At least I'm not at school,* Amy thought. *I hate blushing in front of the whole class!*

In fact Amy wouldn't be back at

her school, Santa Vista Elementary, for one whole week. It was the Friday night before spring break. Amy was in her bedroom with her best friends, Marion, Ellie, and Liz. They had a sleepover almost every Friday. This week, it was Amy's turn to host.

The girls were finishing up a game of MASH. Amy held up the paper that had made her blush. She pointed to the name of her future husband.

Liz, Marion, and Ellie squealed.

"You're so lucky, Amy!" Ellie said, shaking her hands to dry her newly painted nails. Stewart was Liz's big brother. He was twelve. All the girls, except for Liz, thought he was the cutest.

"Lucky?" said Liz. Marion was braiding Liz's wavy blond hair in front of the mirror. Liz wrinkled her nose. "Who would want to marry my *brother*? Ew."

"I can't stay up too late tonight," Marion said. She wrapped a hair band around Liz's braid. "Tomorrow my mom and I are taking Coco to a big horse show!"

Coco was Marion's brown pure-bred horse. Marion was a great rider. Together, Marion and Coco had won tons of blue ribbons! "We'll be out of town for most of the week," Marion added, her green eyes twinkling.

"Me too," said Liz. Liz and her family were going to the beach. "I can't wait! A whole week of sun,

sand, and best of all, no home-work!" Liz flopped back onto Amy's bed. "I'm going to bring my easel and paint box. I'll paint you each a sunset!" Amy loved Liz's paintings. She was such a good artist!

Ellie sighed and fluffed her red pil-low. "Well, I'll be here in Santa Vista *all week,*" she said, plopping down. Her tight black curls bounced over her headband. Ellie tossed her head dramatically. "BOR-ing! But at least my Nana Gloria is coming to stay!"

Ellie's grandmother was moving in with her family. "She's bringing over some boxes—and her parrot, Lenny! I want to teach him a song. Then we can sing a duet!"

Ellie grabbed a pink hairbrush. She flicked on Amy's MP3 player. Singing along with a pop song, Ellie belted into her hairbrush microphone. Ellie always sang loudly and with feeling, like an actress on a stage.

"How about you, Amy?" Ellie said. "What are you going to do this week?"

Amy's heart sank a little. Her friends all had somewhere to go or something to do. She didn't.

Amy's parents were divorced and Amy lived with her mom

in Santa Vista. Her dad lived in Orange Blossom, the next town over. Amy sighed as she remembered that she couldn't even go visit Dad this break because he was away on business.

Amy shrugged. "Read?" she said. "I do have a brand-new Nancy Drew book. Count the change in my piggy bank? Dust my sticker collection?" Her friends giggled, but Amy was only half joking. What *was* she going to do?

"I guess I'll help my mom at

the clinic," Amy said. Amy's mom, Dr. Melanie Purvis, was a veterinarian. She ran a vet clinic in the house next door. Pets from all over Santa Vista came for their checkups. Other times, animals came when they were sick or hurt. Amy loved animals of all kinds. She also loved spending time at her mom's clinic.

As if reading her mind, Amy's cat Milly crawled out from under the bed. She climbed into Amy's lap. "Milly will keep me company. Right, Milly?"

Only seven days until next Friday—their next sleepover. Then they would all be together again.

Oh, well, thought Amy. *Spring break can't last forever.*

chapter 2

A New Friend

Monday morning was slow at the vet clinic. Amy sat behind the front desk. Her mom was busy in back, checking on a sick hamster. Gail, the vet assistant, had gone out for coffee. It looked like Amy was in charge. Normally, being in charge made Amy feel important, but not today. Instead, she wondered what her friends were up to. She sighed. *Nothing ever happens in Santa Vista*, she thought.

Amy looked down at the day's list of appointments.

The next patient wouldn't be there for another fifteen minutes.

APPOINTMENTS

MONDAY

8 Tracy (cocker spaniel): teeth cleaning

9 Cooper (orange tabby): vaccination

10 Rufus (Saint Bernard puppy): 6 month checkup

11 Lulu (Goldfish): ich treatment

12

Amy had already watered
the flower beds out
front, and filled
all the treat jars in
the waiting room with Fitter Critter
healthy pet snacks. Amy tucked the

half-empty bag of treats
into the pocket of her
yellow hoodie.

Since she had
some time to spare,
she decided to read
her book. She put on her purple
reading glasses and opened her
new Nancy Drew mystery.

Nancy started by making a list of suspects. "Who *could* have taken the prize-winning pony from Alice's barn during the night?" she asked herself.

The next-door neighbor, old Mr. Gilbert, came to mind. He sure had been gruff when Nancy met him. Plus, Alice had said that in the whole ten years since she'd moved in, Mr. Gilbert had never once smiled or waved over the fence. Sometimes she felt like Mr. Gilbert didn't want a neighbor at all.

Amy heard a car pull up outside. As she looked out the window, the door of a fancy silver car opened. Amy squinted as a figure stepped out of the car.

Amy gasped. It was none other than *Marge Sullivan*!

Marge Sullivan had lived in Santa Vista for a few years. She lived alone, way out on the edge of town. Her house was huge—like a mansion.

Amy didn't know anyone who had ever been inside it. People said Ms. Sullivan was a billionaire. She hardly ever came into town. When she did, she didn't talk much. Kids and even some parents were afraid of her. Now and then, some brave kids would ring her doorbell on Halloween, but they always ran away before she came to the door.

Amy smoothed her hair and sat up very straight in her chair as

Ms. Sullivan strode in. Ms. Sullivan didn't seem like the kind of person you should slouch around.

The older woman looked down at Amy. It felt like a cold *who-are-you?* look. Amy opened her mouth to speak. But nothing came out! Amy felt the warmth rising in her cheeks. Oh no! She was starting to blush.

All of a sudden, Amy heard the jangle of a dog collar. Around the desk came a blur of brown and white fur. Amy felt a paw on either shoulder as she toppled off her chair. The next thing she knew, she was on the floor and a drooly Saint Bernard puppy was covering her face with doggy kisses.

Amy giggled and squealed. The Fitter Critter treats fell out of her pocket and scattered on to the floor. The puppy sniffed them before he gulped down three.

"Bad boy, Rufus! Naughty!" Ms. Sullivan said sternly. The puppy returned to Ms. Sullivan's side. He sat and looked up at her. His tail was wagging a mile a minute.

Still giggling, Amy picked herself up off the floor. She dried her face with the sleeve of her hoodie.

"Well, it looks like you've made a new friend," Ms. Sullivan said to Amy.

Amy looked up. For a split second, she thought she saw Ms. Sullivan's mouth turn up at the corners. Was at a *smile*? Amy had never seen Sullivan smile before. She'd r seen her with a

before, either.

he thought.

ivan doesn't

like a pet

Just then Dr. Purvis, Amy's
mother, came into the waiting
room. "Hello, Marge! Hello, Rufus!"
she said. She led them to an exam
room.

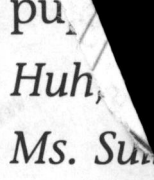

pu

Huh,

Ms. Su

seem

person

with the sleeve of her hoodie.

"Well, it looks like you've made a new friend," Ms. Sullivan said to Amy.

Amy looked up. For a split second, she thought she saw Ms. Sullivan's mouth turn up at the corners. Was that a *smile*? Amy had never seen Ms. Sullivan smile before. She'd never seen her with a puppy before, either. *Huh*, she thought. *Ms. Sullivan doesn't seem like a pet person.*

Just then Dr. Purvis, Amy's mother, came into the waiting room. "Hello, Marge! Hello, Rufus!" she said. She led them to an exam room.

EXAM ROOM #2

Amy looked down at her favorite yellow hoodie. Below each shoulder was one perfect muddy paw print. *Guess Rufus found the wet flower bed on his way in!* Amy thought. She laughed and tried to wipe off the prints with a paper towel. It didn't help.

Rufus had left his mark.

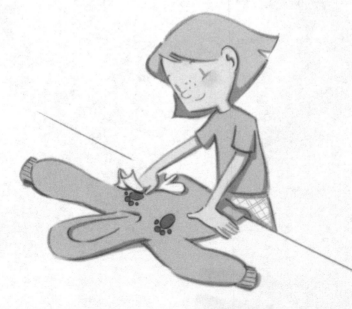

chapter 3

Taking Out the Trash

That night, after dinner, Amy was curled up on the sofa. Her nose was buried deep in the pages of her mystery.

> Nancy followed the small hoofprints across the muddy patch of grass. She could just make them out by the light of the bright, full moon.
>
> Suddenly, Nancy heard a rustling coming from the trees!

She froze. Lifting her flashlight, she aimed the beam into the woods. There it was again! The rustling grew louder and louder, until . . .

Branches parted and the flashlight beam lit up a face— the face of a man. Nancy gasped. It was Mr. Gilbert!

"Amy!" Amy's mom called from the kitchen. "Please come take out the trash!"

Amy sighed and put her book down. "Coming!" she called. She hurried into the kitchen. The faster she took out the trash, the sooner she could get back to her book! She grabbed the full trash bag and dashed out the back door.

Amy didn't bother to turn on the backyard light. She lifted the metal trash can lid and dumped the bag inside. Amy dropped the lid, letting it crash down with a loud *bang*.

Then, she heard it. Amy *thought* she heard a rustling sound! She could have sworn it came from the shrubs between her backyard and the clinic next door. Amy peered into the dark, shadowy shrubs, but couldn't see anything. She stood still, listening. Nothing.

Then the wind picked up. Shrubs and tree branches waved. Leaves rustled. Amy thought the air smelled like rain.

Amy relaxed. Her book was putting ideas into her head!

Back inside, Amy found her mom on the sofa with a big bowl of popcorn. "Want to watch that new spy movie?" Dr. Purvis asked.

Amy smiled. No school tomorrow meant no bedtime. Amy flopped down on the sofa. She could read her book later. Movie night with her mom was the best.

Outside, the first few raindrops
tapped against the windows.

41

A Surprise Guest

Halfway through the movie, the doorbell rang. Dr. Purvis pressed pause on the remote control. "Who could that be?" she said. "It's kind of late . . ."

Amy followed her to the front door. She stood next to her mom as she opened it.

Just then a streak of lightning lit

up the dark sky. Thunder clapped. Amy jumped. She grabbed the back of her mom's sweater.

Marge Sullivan was standing on the front porch.

Water dripped from her rain hat. Her black raincoat was soaked. Her cheeks even looked wet. Amy realized it wasn't from the rain. Ms. Sullivan was crying.

"I'm really sorry to bother you," Ms. Sullivan said to Dr. Purvis. "It's Rufus. He's . . . gone!"

Amy's mom invited her in. Amy's heart was still pounding in

her chest, but she followed as her mom led the way to the kitchen. Dr. Purvis took Ms. Sullivan's wet things. Ms. Sullivan had a seat at the table.

"I'll make you some tea," said Dr. Purvis as she put the kettle on. "You tell us what happened."

Amy stood in the doorway and listened.

"I let Rufus out after dinner," Ms. Sullivan began. "The backyard is fenced in.

"When it got windy, I called him in," Ms. Sullivan went on, "but Rufus didn't come. When I went out to look for him, I found a hole by the fence. He must have dug it out."

Ms. Sullivan's lower lip shook. "My poor Rufus. He's out in this storm, all alone."

Dr. Purvis put a hand on Ms. Sullivan's shoulder. "He can't have gotten far," she said. "Let me make some phone calls." She took her cell phone and left the room.

Amy didn't know what to say or do. Ms. Sullivan had always seemed stern and serious. Now, here she was crying in Amy's kitchen. When the kettle whistled, Amy made her a cup of tea. She set it on the table with the milk and sugar.

"Thank you, Amy," Ms. Sullivan said softly. Amy was surprised Ms. Sullivan knew her name.

Dr. Purvis came back in. "Well, I called the police. I also called the animal shelter over in Orange Blossom. If they hear anything or spot Rufus, they'll let us know right away." Dr. Purvis sighed. "It's really a shame Santa Vista doesn't have its own animal shelter."

Dr. Purvis and Ms. Sullivan talked a while longer. Amy went upstairs. As she got ready for bed, she could hear her mother and Ms. Sullivan in the front hall. "I'll help you look in the morning, Marge," her mom was saying. "He'll be easier to spot in the daylight."

Amy heard the front door close. As she opened her book, she wondered how Nancy Drew would solve this mystery.

Clues . . . , thought Amy. *Rufus must have left some clues behind.* If Amy could find them, maybe *she* could help find Rufus. It would be Amy's first case.

The First Clue!

By Tuesday morning the storm had passed. The sun was warm as Amy walked next door. She'd help out at the clinic for the morning. Then, she'd call Ellie. She missed her friends so much!

How many times have I walked down this sidewalk? Amy wondered. *A million times?* That's how she knew there were fifteen sidewalk squares between the two houses. She counted them in her head as she walked.

But this morning, on square number nine, Amy stopped in her tracks.

Right there on the sidewalk were several paw prints. Amy felt like she had seen one exactly like it yesterday. Amy

remembered
the paw prints
on her favorite
yellow hoodie!

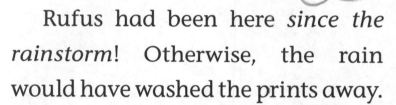

Rufus had been here *since the rainstorm*! Otherwise, the rain would have washed the prints away.

Amy smiled. This was a clue! But now what? What would Nancy Drew do? And then she knew.

Amy hurried back into her house. She returned with a small green notebook and her favorite blue pen. She opened the notebook and began to write.

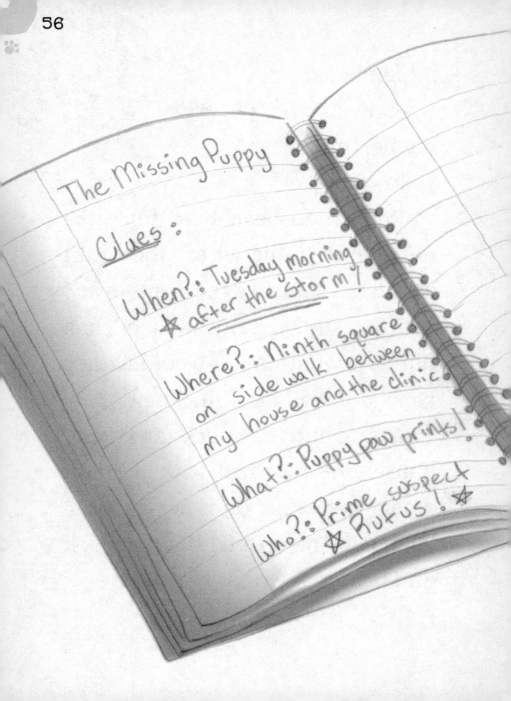

It was a start! Amy was on her way to solving the mystery of the missing puppy!

Rufus Was Here

Amy was in charge at the front desk all morning while her mom and Ms. Sullivan were out looking for Rufus. Gail, the vet assistant, was busy giving some checkups while Amy watered the flower bed out front and refilled the treat jars.

Dr. Purvis finally returned around lunchtime.

"Any luck?" Amy asked her.

Her mom shook her head no. "We drove all over. No sign of him."

Amy pulled out her notebook. "I found one sign of him," she said. She explained how the print on the sidewalk matched the Rufus prints on her hoodie.

Amy's mom smiled. "Great detective work!" she said. "The more people looking, the better chance we have of finding Rufus."

Amy walked home and had lunch. After she finished her sandwich, she called Ellie's house.

"Amy!" Ellie cried when she came to the phone. "Am I glad to hear from you!" There was really loud squawking in the background. "Nana Gloria's parrot is driving me nuts!"

Amy couldn't make out Lenny the parrot's words. But it sounded like he was singing a song. Well, if you could call all that squawking *singing*.

Amy told Ellie about Rufus going missing. She also told Ellie about the paw print. "Do you want to come over?" Amy asked. "We could look for more clues together."

The words were barely out of Amy's mouth. Ellie shouted, "I'll be right over!" and hung up.

Ellie lived only three streets
over. A few minutes later, she rode
up on her bike. Amy went outside
to meet her.

"Oh, Amy," Ellie said, giving her
a hug. She was out of breath. "I love
Lenny, but that bird does not stop
talking *or* singing!"

Amy held back a giggle. She knew Ellie didn't think it was funny.

Amy told Ellie all about the case: how Rufus got loose, when he went missing, and what he looked like. She showed Ellie the paw prints on

the sidewalk. Together, they looked around for more.

"Here!" Ellie said, pointing at the sidewalk. They were past the clinic. A trail of paw prints led further down the sidewalk.

"Yes! Rufus prints, for sure!" Amy cried. She pulled out her notebook and jotted down these clues.

The girls slowly followed the trail. "I don't blame Rufus for running away from mean old Ms. Sullivan," said Ellie "I would run away too!"

They were in front of the house on the other side of the clinic. The paw prints were disappearing.

"I don't know," Amy replied. She thought about how sad Ms. Sullivan was about losing Rufus. It was clear she really loved him. "Maybe Ms. Sullivan isn't as bad as everyone thinks. You know what they say about judging a book by its cover."

Ellie stopped walking. She looked at Amy. She rolled her eyes. "You *would* talk about books at a time like this, Amy."

The girls looked down. Suddenly

there were no more paw prints.
They were at a dead end.

"Now what?" Ellie said.

Amy looked down at her notebook. She turned to a blank page.

"If we were Rufus, where would
we go?" asked Amy.

They thought about it as they
walked back to Amy's house. They

decided they would spend the rest
of the afternoon making a new list.

Places to Check

1. Park

2. Dog Run

3. Pet Store

4. Bakery (for the smells!)

5. Behind Grocery Store

At four thirty Ellie eyed the clock
and jumped up. "I've got to go," she

said. "Nana Gloria is making dinner, and I promised her I'd help."

The girls made plans to meet up the next day. "I'll be at the clinic all morning," Amy said, "but after lunch, we should check these places."

Ellie nodded. "That sounds much better than hanging out with crazy Lenny all day!"

chapter 7

Follow That Puppy!

The next day Amy rode her bike to Ellie's house. Together she and Ellie pedaled toward the park. It was the first place on their list.

"Can you believe today is Wednesday?" Ellie called to Amy. "Spring break is already halfway over!"

Ellie was right! *Wow!* thought

Amy. She had imagined spending the entire week *reading* a mystery. *Time sure does fly when you're* solving *one!*

On their way to the park, Amy and Ellie passed Liz's house. Amy was shocked to see Liz's family's van in the driveway. "Look!" Amy called. "Liz is back early!"

As the girls parked their bikes, Liz came out of the house. "Yay! Liz!" Ellie cried.

The three girls hugged. "You're back early!" Amy said.

Liz nodded. "We had to cut our beach trip short thanks to Stewart's sunburn. So long, sun and sand . . . and all because *he* forgot to put on sunscreen!"

Stewart was coming around the side of the house. "I heard that!" he said. Stewart's face, arms, and legs were bright red like a tomato.

"Hi, Stewart!" Ellie shouted cheerfully. She gave him a funny little wave.

Stewart was too grumpy to notice. "This day gets worse and worse," he said. "Three hours in the car, sitting on sunburned legs, and now I get pawed by some stray puppy! Man, that really hurt!"

Stewart turned. There, on his shorts, were two muddy paw prints! Amy and Ellie stared. Rufus prints!

They crowded around Stewart. "What puppy?" Amy asked.

"Where?" Ellie cried. "Which way did he go?"

Stewart looked confused. "A Saint Bernard, I think,"

he said. He pointed toward the backyard. "He ran that way."

Amy and Ellie dashed around the side of Liz's house. Liz followed. "Wait up!" she shouted. "What's going on?"

Amy didn't have time to explain.

She and Ellie got to the backyard—
just in time to spot Rufus!

Right before he disappeared
under the fence.

Amy and Ellie dashed over.
"RUFUS!" they shouted. The girls
peeked through the fence to watch
Rufus run through the neighbor's

yard. In seconds, he was gone.

Liz caught up. She looked over the fence too. "Who was that?" she asked.

"Come on," said Amy. "We'll fill you in."

The three girls hurried to the clinic. Amy wanted to tell her mom they'd seen Rufus! On the way, Amy and Ellie told Liz about

Ms. Sullivan's missing puppy.

"Hi, girls!" said Dr. Purvis when she saw them. She was out back by the supply shed. "Hey, Amy, have you seen that new case of Fitter Critter treats?"

Amy remembered it had been delivered the other day. "I put it here by the shed door."

"Huh," Amy's mom said, looking around. "Maybe Gail moved it." She looked at Amy. "So, what's up?"

The girls told her about seeing Rufus in Liz's backyard. Dr. Purvis was excited! "That means Rufus is still in the area and he's okay!" she said. "That's great news!"

Dr. Purvis suggested they put up MISSING PUPPY flyers around town. "I believe one of you loves to draw . . . ?"

Ellie and Amy looked at Liz. She grinned.

The girls worked together. Amy described what Rufus looked like while Liz did the drawing. Amy decided what the flyer should say. Ellie picked an eye-catching shade of hot pink paper for the flyers. They finished just as Dr. Purvis was locking up the clinic for the day.

MISSING PUPPY

Fluffy, brown and white St. Bernard, responds to Rufus. Please contact Santa Vista Vet Clinic if found. Thank You!

"Are you guys busy tomorrow?" Amy asked her friends. She would need help putting up the flyers.

Ellie and Liz smiled. "We are now!" Liz said.

A New Lead

Dr. Purvis made copies of the flyer on the clinic's photocopier. Then Amy, Ellie, and Liz spent all day Thursday handing them out. They started with number one on their list of places to check—the park.

Ellie taped a flyer to the notice board by the playground. Meanwhile, Amy checked the field.

Liz looked over by the water fountain for pets. There was no sign of Rufus anywhere.

Next on the list was the dog run.

The girls handed a few flyers to dog owners. No one had seen Rufus, but everyone said they'd look out for him.

The girls headed over to the pet store on Main Street. "I walk by here with Sam sometimes," Ellie said. Sam was her family's golden retriever. "He always stops and barks like crazy."

Amy wasn't surprised. There were always cats in the front window. Today there were some beautiful tabby cats and three cute black-and-white kittens.

Amy froze. There was also something else: a muddy paw print, right on the window glass! "Aha!" she said, pointing.

The girls spoke to the pet store owner. They gave her a flyer. She remembered a dog that looked like Rufus. "Yesterday afternoon. I saw him out front, all alone. When I went to check on him, he ran off. I haven't seen him since."

Amy wrote down the info in her notebook. The girls thanked the

owner and headed for number four on their list, the bakery.

The smell of baking bread and cakes made Amy's mouth water. She'd bet a hungry dog could smell this place from miles away, but no

one at the bakery had seen Rufus.

They hung up more flyers: at the grocery store, the post office, the café, and on every bulletin board downtown.

But they didn't find another clue, until . . .

"What's that?" Ellie asked. Amy had stopped on the town square. She was bending over a piece of trash on the grass.

"Good for you, Amy," said Liz. "We should all do

our part to keep the Earth clean."
Liz and her family were really into
the environment. "Want me to toss
that?"

"No, wait. Know what this is?"
Amy said. She held up the piece of
trash. It was an empty bag of Fitter
Critter treats. "And look here." Amy

pointed to one corner. "It's chewed open."

Ellie and Liz understood and nodded. "By a hungry puppy?" Ellie said.

Amy wrote down the clue in her notebook. The list now took up two pages. There had to be *something* the clues could tell them?

"So, here's what we know," Amy said. She sat down under a shady tree. Ellie and Liz sat down

next to her. "Rufus is leaving paw prints everywhere."

"He's been to the pet store," Ellie added, "and Liz's yard . . . and in front of the clinic . . ."

"His prints are always muddy," said Liz, "even though it hasn't rained since Monday."

"Right!" said Amy. "Hmm. Someplace that's always wet . . . ?" She held up the empty treat bag. "And where did Rufus find these?"

The clues and the events of the last week swirled in Amy's mind.

Then it hit her! Lightbulbs went

off in her head. That case of Fitter Critter treats her mom was looking for . . . The flower bed at the clinic, watered every morning . . . The rustling sound she'd heard from her backyard Monday night . . .

"Of course!" Amy shouted. "I think I know where to find Rufus!" She jumped up and led the girls toward the clinic.

Amy had a plan.

chapter 9

Gotcha!

On Friday morning Amy slowly and quietly ate her cereal. Her mom sipped her coffee. She looked across the table at Amy. "Nothing yet?" she asked.

"Nope," Amy said, shaking her head. "Not yet—"

Clatter, clatter, CRASH! came a noise from outside. Amy's eyes brightened. She jumped up from the table.

Dr. Purvis rushed to look out the back window. "It's Rufus!" she cried. She grabbed the leash they had ready. Together, they darted out the back door.

Rufus was by the metal trash can, which had been knocked over. The lid was off, and a very muddy Rufus was slurping Fitter Critter treats off the driveway. Quickly, Dr. Purvis clipped the leash to his collar.

"Hooray!" Dr. Purvis cheered.

"Amy, I'm so proud of you! Your plan really worked!"

Amy grinned. She felt proud of her plan too. The clues had got her

to thinking. Had Rufus been hanging around the clinic the whole
time? On Thursday afternoon Amy
and her friends had searched all
around the clinic. They didn't find

Rufus, but they did find what was left of the missing case of Fitter Critter treats. They also found lots and lots of Rufus prints.

The girls put a plan in motion. They took a package of Fitter Critters and left a trail of treats leading to Amy's trash can. They put a bunch of treats on the lid so when Rufus jumped up to get them . . . *CRASH!*

"It worked perfectly!" Amy cried.

"Ms. Sullivan will be so happy!" her mom said. "I'll go call her. And then . . ." She looked down at Rufus and pinched her nose.

Amy smelled it too. "Woof . . . Rufus needs a bath!"

Ms. Sullivan's Idea

Amy called Liz and Ellie from the clinic. Liz came over right away. Ellie arrived next. "Look who I found on the way," she said. Marion came in behind her. She held up her blue ribbon. She and Coco had won first place at the horse show! Amy, Liz, and Ellie crowded around her for a group hug.

Rufus ran in from the other room. He put two muddy front paws on Marion's knees. Marion patted him on the head. "Hiya, Rufus," she said. "Ellie was just telling me all about you . . . *and* your muddy paws!"

Rufus wagged his tail. And it didn't stop wagging as the girls splashed, soaped, rinsed, dried, and brushed him.

When they were done, Rufus was one clean and happy dog.

"Wait!" said Marion. "He needs a little something extra." She tied her blue ribbon to Rufus's collar. "Perfect!"

"Awwww," said Amy. "Nice touch, Marion."

"I agree," said Dr. Purvis from the hallway. "Girls, Ms. Sullivan is in the waiting room. How about we bring her this handsome pup?"

Amy noticed her friends looked a little nervous. "Don't worry, guys," she said. "You'll like Ms. Sullivan."

Rufus led the way. He ran right to Ms. Sullivan. She knelt down with her arms wide open. Rufus jumped up and licked her face over and over. She hugged him tight and smiled from ear to ear. "My Rufus!" she cried. "Oh, thank you, Dr. Purvis, and thank you, girls! Amy, your mom told me how you tracked Rufus down. I can't even tell you how grateful I am."

Amy could feel herself blushing, but she didn't mind. "Glad to help, Ms. Sullivan," Amy said quietly.

Ms. Sullivan stood up. "I want to ask you and your friends for help with something else. I was just discussing it with your mom." Dr. Purvis nodded.

"After this Rufus adventure, I've decided that I want to open an animal shelter here in Santa Vista," Ms. Sullivan went on. "I have a big barn that's empty and isn't being used. I thought it might be the perfect spot."

Amy gasped. "What a great idea!" she cried.

Ms. Sullivan smiled. "I'm so glad you think so, Amy. I can't do it alone. I mean, I do have the money and the barn. Dr. Purvis has kindly offered to be the veterinarian for the shelter, but there will be lots of other work to do. Feeding and taking care of the animals . . ." Ms. Sullivan looked at all the girls. "Would you four mind helping me get it started?"

The girls looked at one another, wide-eyed. *"Mind?"* cried Marion.

"Are you serious?" asked Liz.

"It's the most exciting thing that's ever happened to me!" cried Ellie.

Amy jumped up and down. "We'd love to!"

Dr. Purvis smiled at the girls. "Ms. Sullivan, I think you have a deal."

The End and the Beginning

That night the girls were all sitting around Liz's bedroom. It was Friday night and there was time for one more sleepover before spring break was over.

"What a week!" said Liz, drawing in her sketch pad. "That was the shortest beach vacation I've ever had. Thanks to Stewart."

Ellie was pecking out a tune on Liz's electronic keyboard. "Yeah, spring break was not long enough. At least Lenny's singing is getting better," she said, rolling her eyes.

Marion had brought her scrap-book. She was adding photos from

the horse show. "I had a blast at the show," she said, "but I feel like I missed all the fun here!"

It was a fun week in Santa Vista, Amy thought. She'd been so busy that she hadn't had time to finish her Nancy Drew book! Amy looked down at the last page.

> At last, all the clues added up. Nancy could prove that Sandy Jessup had taken the pony. But if Sandy wouldn't admit it, how would Nancy ever find the pony?
>
> Just then, there was a knock at Alice's door. Nancy stood by Alice's side as she opened it. Standing on Alice's front porch was Mr. Gilbert—with the pony!
>
> "I believe this little lady belongs to you?" Mr. Gilbert said. His tone was as gruff as ever, but Nancy could swear she saw a twinkle in his eye.

"That reminds me," said Amy. "Isn't Ms. Sullivan the best?"

The girls all agreed. "You were right, Amy," said Ellie. "We were judging the book by its cover."

"She's not at all what I thought," said Marion. "Can you believe she let us pick the name for the shelter?"

Liz turned her sketch pad around. "Look!" she said. "I drew

up an ad. Maybe we could get it in next week's edition of the *Santa Vista Star*?"

"The Critter Club!" Marion read Liz's poster. "I love the name we came up with," she said happily.

Everyone else nodded.

"I bet Rufus will like the name too!" said Ellie. "It sounds a lot like Fitter Critters, his favorite treat!"

Amy laughed. "As long as we stock the barn with those treats, Rufus won't care *what* we call it!"

She smiled, thinking about all

the other animals that The Critter Club would help. Spring break was almost over, but it felt like the beginning of a big, new adventure.

125

the CRITTER club

🐾 All About Ellie 🐾

Table of Contents

Chapter 1   Starring . . . Ellie!   131

Chapter 2   Ellie Takes the Stage   145

Chapter 3   VIBs: Very Important Bunnies   153

Chapter 4   One-Track Mind   165

Chapter 5   Preshow Jitters!   173

Chapter 6   Ellie's Fan Club   181

Chapter 7   A Bad Kind of Drama   187

Chapter 8   An Ellie Sometimes Forgets   197

Chapter 9   A Secret Movie Star   209

Chapter 10   Making Things Right   225

Chapter 11   Bravo, Ellie!   235

Chapter 1

Starring . . . Ellie!

"Okay," said Ellie, kneeling on her bed. "Here's what I planned for us to do tonight!"

Her best friends, Liz, Amy, and Marion, had just arrived. Ellie was so excited. It was Friday and her turn to host their weekly sleepover.

"First I can teach you this really cool dance I learned in tap class,"

Ellie began. "And after that we can put on the play we made up at Liz's house! And—"

"Ellie, hold on," Liz said with a giggle. "We just got here!"

"Yeah," agreed Marion. She unrolled her sleeping bag. "All that sounds fun, but maybe we could relax and talk first?"

Ellie's face fell a little. She'd been looking forward to this sleepover for . . . well, *forever*. After all, she only got a turn to host every four weeks, and being the host was special. It meant planning everything and being at the center of it all!

"Oh!" said Amy. "We have some Critter Club stuff to talk about. Remember?"

Ellie got excited again. "The bunnies!" she cried.

"Right," said Amy. "Our first

animals at The Critter Club!"

Ellie and her friends had been working hard to get The Critter Club up and running. A few weeks ago it was an empty barn belonging to Ms. Sullivan, their new friend. Now, with the help of Amy's mom, veterinarian Dr. Purvis, it was an animal shelter. It had all been Ms. Sullivan's idea!

Before The Critter Club the girls thought Ms. Sullivan was kind of mean, but they'd been totally wrong. When Ms. Sullivan's puppy Rufus had gone missing, the girls helped her find him. That's when The Critter Club was born!

"You still don't know who left the bunnies?" Marion asked Amy.

Amy shook her head no. "There was no note," Amy replied. "Just

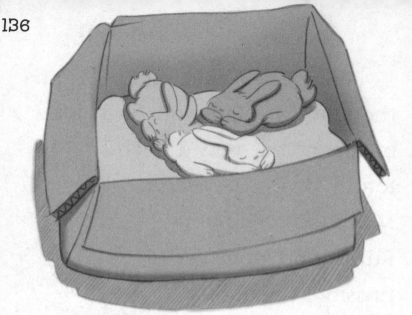

three baby bunnies in a card-
board box."

"Poor things!" said Ellie. "How
could someone just leave them?"

Amy shrugged. "Mom thinks
someone's pet rabbit had babies,
and they couldn't take care of
them all."

"Well, speaking of taking care of them," said Marion, pulling out a notebook, "we should make a schedule." Marion was super organized. She was always writing things down and making lists.

Ellie hopped off her bed. She sat on the floor next to Marion. In her notebook Marion made a chart.

"So we'll take turns," said Marion. "Each day after school two of us will go feed the bunnies and give them water. Amy's mom and Ms. Sullivan will handle the morning shifts."

All the girls agreed. Liz picked up a pen. She drew three little bunnies below the chart.

"We have to find good homes for them," Ellie said. "They're counting on us, and we can't let them down!" Then she jumped up. "Okay, now, on to other things . . ."

Ellie ducked behind her hot-pink window curtains. She peeked out at her friends. "Who's trying out for the spring play?" she asked.

Their school, Santa Vista Elementary,

put on a play every year. This year's musical was called *Miss Ladybug Saves Spring.*

"We should all try out!" Ellie cried excitedly.

"Not me," said Liz. "I'm finishing my painting for that big art contest, remember?" Liz was an amazing artist. "Plus, you guys know I can't sing!" she added with a laugh.

Marion pulled her long brown hair into a ponytail. "I'm way

too busy too," she said. "Homework plus piano lessons three times a week!"

Ellie sighed. "How about you, Amy?" she asked. But Ellie knew what Amy was about to say.

"Me? Get on stage? In front of *people*? And *dance*? No way," Amy said, shaking her head.

Liz smiled a little smile. "How about you, Ellie? Are *you* going to try out?"

"YES!!!" Ellie squealed. She

jumped out from behind the curtain. "I can't wait! Have you seen the stage? It's sooooo big! Do you think they'll have the spotlight on for auditions? Oh! What should I wear? What song should I sing? You guys have to help me decide!"

Liz, Marion, and Amy laughed. They settled in, happy to be Ellie's audience. Ellie was so glad they were there to cheer her on and help her prepare.

After all, that's what friends were for. Right?

Chapter 2

Ellie Takes the Stage

Backstage at the school auditorium, Ellie looked at herself in the mirror. It was the big day, and Ellie was next on the list. Mrs. Jameson, the teacher who ran drama club, would call her name any minute to audition for the lead role! That part almost always went to a third grader, but Ellie felt she *had* to try for it anyway. Obviously, Miss Ladybug's costume would be red. *Red is totally my color!* thought Ellie.

"Ellie Mitchell," she said to herself, "this is your chance." She fluffed her hair and smoothed her red dress. All her life—all eight years— she had wanted to be a star. At two years old, she dressed up and did shows for her mom and dad. At three years old, she started dance classes. She remembered a video her mom took of her first tap recital. In it she had bumped into another girl to be in the spotlight.

Just then Ellie heard Mrs. Jameson calling. "Ellie! Ellie Mitchell!"

It was time for her to take center stage. Getting the lead role would be her dream come true! "You can do this!" Ellie told herself. She hurried onstage.

The stage lights were bright. Squinting, Ellie could make out Mrs. Jameson in the front row. She saw someone waving from the back row.

It was Liz! And Marion and Amy were next to her! They had come to

cheer her on! *Aw, that's so sweet of them,* thought Ellie. *They're such great friends.*

"Hello, Ellie," Mrs. Jameson said kindly. "Whenever you are ready, I'd love to hear your audition song."

Ellie took a deep breath. Her eyes locked on Liz, Marion, and Amy.

She pretended she was in her own bedroom and that she was singing to them—just to them. The next moment she was lost in the song. Her voice filled the auditorium as she moved to the music. She even threw in some twirls, leaps, and hand motions.

It was over before Ellie knew it. Her last note hung in the air, ringing clear and strong.

Then another sound filled the air—a wonderful sound. Applause! In the back row Liz, Marion, and Amy were clapping like crazy. Ellie took a bow and waved at her friends.

Chapter 3

VIBs:
Very Important Bunnies

The next day after school the girls walked together to Mrs. Jameson's classroom. She had posted the cast list outside her door. It listed the role each person had been given.

There was Ellie's name, right at the top!

Miss Ladybug Saves Spring	
~ Role ~	~ Student ~
Miss Ladybug	Ellie Mitchell
Bumblebee 1	Steven Connor
Bumblebee 2	Karlie Lemon
Flower Dancer 1	Marjorie Jones

153

Ellie was so excited and surprised! She was speechless.
She—a second grader—would
star as Miss Ladybug, the biggest
role in the whole play!

Liz, Marion, and Amy each gave
her a big hug. "Way to go, Ellie!"
Liz squealed.

Ellie was in heaven. She was so happy she felt like she was walking on air. Then it slowly began to dawn on her: She had so much to do to get ready for the show!

• • • • • • • • • • • • • • • • • • • •

Weeks flew by in a flash. Ellie had never felt so busy before.

Each school day during lunch hour, Mrs. Jameson held short rehearsals in the auditorium. Every Wednesday after school, they had a longer rehearsal.

Ellie also had Critter Club duty two days a week after school. On

Mondays she went with Liz. On Thursdays she and Amy went together.

It was enough to make Ellie's head spin! Luckily, Marion had made Ellie a schedule. She kept it taped to the front of her homework folder.

And that was just weekdays! On Saturdays and Sundays all four girls met at The Critter Club to feed the bunnies and clean the big rabbit hutch.

One sunny Saturday morning they were all in the barn. Marion

Weekly Schedule

Monday	Play rehearsal at lunchtime
	Critter Club with Liz in the afternoon
Tuesday	Play rehearsal at lunchtime
	After-school Dance!
Wednesday	Play rehearsal at lunchtime
	Play rehearsal (long one) after school
Thursday	Play rehearsal at lunchtime
	Critter Club with Amy in the afternoon
Friday	Play rehearsal at lunchtime
	Sleepover!!! Yay! ☆☆

sat on the floor with the bunnies
playing around her.

"Is *that* the one we named
Floppy?" Ellie asked, pointing to a
gray bunny.

"No, that's Fluffy," said Amy.

She was hosing down the inside of the hutch. "The other gray one is Floppy."

"Which other gray one?" asked Ellie. She opened a bag of wood shavings to make fresh bedding. "Aren't they all gray?"

Liz giggled as she swept around

the rabbit hutch. "No, Frosty is silvery white. The light gray one is Fluffy. And the steel gray one is Floppy."

Marion and Amy laughed. "Leave it to the artist to have three different names for the same color!" Marion said.

Ellie felt badly that she hadn't known which bunny was which. She hadn't been there when Amy's mom had given the bunnies full checkups. Dr. Purvis had also taught the other girls the basics of caring for them. Bunnies loved to be petted. They were calm and gentle, but their nails could be sharp. Bunnies sometimes chewed on things they shouldn't. The girls could give them special chew toys

or carrots to chew instead.

Amy's mom said that people looking for a new pet might not even think of rabbits. It was up to The Critter Club to change that and find homes for their furry friends!

But right now all Ellie could think about was how much more play practice she needed.

163

Chapter 4

One-Track Mind

There was so much going on! Ellie made sure to keep her friends up to date on *everything*. She jumped at any chance to tell them *all* about the play.

One morning Ellie was walking to school with Amy. Amy was talking about her weekend at her dad's house in Orange Blossom. Orange

Blossom was a bigger city near Santa Vista.

Meanwhile Ellie had a thought. She wanted to tell Amy about her costume for the play. It had long, flowing sleeves that looked like ladybug wings. The red fabric looked glittery under the lights. When Ellie twirled around the stage . . .

"Ellie? Hello? Ellie?" Amy was saying.

"Oh, huh?" Ellie replied. "What did you say?"

"I was telling you all about my weekend at my dad's," Amy said. "It was really—"

"I'm *so* sorry, Amy!" Ellie jumped in. "I was thinking about my costume for the play!" She went on to tell Amy everything about her costume from head to toe.

Ellie saw Amy roll her eyes. She wasn't sure why. Maybe Amy had something *in* her eye? So Ellie kept on talking. She made sure not to leave anything out.

Another day Ellie was on the phone with Liz. "I forgot our reading book at school," Liz said. "Can I borrow yours?"

"Sure!" Ellie replied. "Come over! While you're here, I can read you my lines from the play! And you haven't heard my part in the opening song! I'll sing that for you

too. *And* I've got to tell you what happened at rehearsal today!"

"Um, actually," Liz said, "I bet Amy has her book at home. Her house is closer. I'll borrow hers. Thanks." And she hung up. *Guess she's in a hurry to do her homework,* thought Ellie.

Two days later at Marion's house,

Marion was telling Ellie a story about her horse, Coco. Right in the middle of it, Marion stopped. "Ellie, are you even listening?" she asked.

"What?" said Ellie. "What do you mean?"

"Well, you were humming," Marion said, "while I was talking."

"I was?" Ellie said. She *had* been thinking about a song from the play. She didn't realize she'd been singing it *out loud*. Ellie giggled. "Oops. It's just a song from the play. Want to hear it?"

Marion frowned. "Oh," she said. "Yes. *My* story can wait. Let's hear *your* song."

"Okay!" said Ellie, and she began to sing. If her friends couldn't be in the play with her, she was glad she could tell them all about it!

"Ladybug Sunshine, la, la, la!"

Chapter 5

Preshow Jitters!

The next Friday before school Ellie checked the calendar. The play was exactly one week away!

At school, before the morning bell, the girls met up on the play- ground. "Do you know what today is?" Ellie asked them.

"Yep!" said Liz. "Friday!"

"We have a sleepover tonight!"

Amy cheered. "Marion, it's at your house, right?"

Marion nodded and opened her mouth to speak. But Ellie blurted out, "No! Not that! I mean, the play! The play is in *one* week—one week from *today*!"

Liz put her arm around Ellie. "Don't worry," she said in a calm tone. "You're going to be great."

"You're totally ready," said Marion.

"We've heard all the lines to all the songs . . . ," said Amy. "You *definitely* know them by heart!"

Ellie smiled. "I know, I know," she said. "Oh yeah! I almost forgot to tell you guys. I can't make it to the sleepover tonight."

"What?" Liz asked, surprised. "Why not?"

Ellie sat down on a swing. "I really need to use *all* my spare time to prepare for the show— study my lines, and rehearse my songs, and get a ton of rest," said Ellie. "It's going to be a busy weekend. We have an extra rehearsal tomorrow morning. Then my mom is taking me to Orange Blossom to pick up my specially made costume!" Going shopping in Orange Blossom was always a special treat.

"Wait," said Amy. "So you're not coming to the sleepover *and* you won't be at The Critter Club tomorrow?"

177

The Critter Club! thought Ellie, remembering. She shook her head and shrugged. "I can't make it," she said. "It's just . . . the play is only *a week away*. Just *seven days*."

Marion rolled her eyes. "Uh, yeah. You mentioned *that*."

Just then the bell rang. Everyone had to line up to go inside. That got Ellie thinking. At the end of the play would the cast line up to take a bow together? Or would they each get to take their own bow? She had to ask Mrs. Jameson about that at rehearsal.

Ellie's Fan Club

"Ellie!" called Mrs. Mitchell. "Time for dinner!"

It was Sunday evening. In her room Ellie sighed. She dropped her script and went downstairs. She stood next to her seat at the dining room table. Ellie's mom, dad, little brother Toby, and Nana Gloria were already there, waiting for her.

"Mom, I don't have time to eat," Ellie said.

"Oh, come on, Ellie," her mom replied. "You have to eat *something*."

"Your mother's right," said Nana Gloria. "You need to keep up your strength. Otherwise you'll never make it to Friday's showtime!" She

winked and smiled at Ellie. Ellie smiled back. She was so happy Nana Gloria had come to live with them a few weeks ago. Already, Ellie couldn't remember what the house was like without her. She always gave good advice.

Her dad picked up a covered dish. "You've been going nonstop all weekend, Ellie," he said. "So sit, relax, and eat. We made your favorite." He whisked the lid off the dish.

"Chicken pot pie!" Ellie cried. *Mmm,* she thought. *I am kind of hungry.* She sat down next to Toby.

"Yummy!" said Toby, picking up his fork.

"Bravo!" came a squawky voice from the corner. Everyone laughed and looked at Nana Gloria's parrot, Lenny, perched in his cage. Ellie and Lenny had become good pals. Ellie had taught him to say "Bravo!" after she sang and danced.

"Can Lenny come to the play, please?" asked Toby. "And Sam, too?" Sam was their golden retriever. Toby didn't like going places without Sam.

Ellie laughed at the thought of barks and a squawky "Bravo!" mixed in with the applause. "I don't think so, Toby," she said.

Plus, adorable critters would totally steal the spotlight! Ellie thought.

Squawk!

Squawk!

A Bad Kind of Drama

On Monday at school, Ellie spotted Amy and Marion heading into the classroom. "Guys! Wait up!" she called and hurried over.

"Oh, hey, Ellie," Marion said flatly.

"Hi," said Amy.

They both sounded kind of bored to Ellie. They kept on walking.

"Hey, what's up?" Ellie said excitedly. "I haven't seen you guys all weekend! How was the sleepover? How was Saturday at The Critter Club?" Ellie went on without really waiting for an answer. "Boy, what a crazy weekend I had! Rehearsal, costume fitting, studying my lines—"

"That's nice, Ellie," Marion said in the same flat voice.

"Yeah, sounds great," said Amy.

That's funny, thought Ellie. *They don't sound like they think it's nice and great.*

Their teacher, Mrs. Sienna, asked everyone to take their seats. Without another word Amy and Marion crossed the room. They sat at their desks by the window. Ellie saw Liz already in her seat by the bookshelf. Ellie waved. Liz waved back, but didn't smile. *That's not like Liz,* thought Ellie.

I wonder if she's feeling okay.

Ellie sat down at her desk near the classroom door. Soon Mrs. Sienna got them started on morning math, but Ellie couldn't concentrate on fractions. She kept looking over at her friends. They all had their noses in their work. Ellie tried to catch their attention, but none of

them looked her way all morning.

It was almost lunchtime when there was a knock on the class-room door. Mrs. Sienna answered it. A fifth grader gave the teacher a folded piece of paper. "Liz," she said after reading it, "the principal would like to see you."

Ellie looked at Liz. She looked surprised. "Right now?" Liz asked.

"Yes, right now," said Mrs. Sienna.

"Take your lunch. You can go straight to the cafeteria afterward."

Uh-oh, thought Ellie. *What's up?* She watched Liz get her lunch from her backpack. Then she walked out of the classroom.

Ten long minutes later the lunch

bell rang. Ellie jumped out of her seat, got out her lunch bag, and headed for the door. Ellie wanted to talk to Marion and Amy. She caught up to them in the hallway.

"Guys," she said, "is everything okay with Liz?"

Marion and Amy kept on walking. Ellie thought they hadn't heard her.

"Guys?" Ellie tried again.

Marion stopped and turned to Ellie. "Oh! Are you speaking to us, *superstar*?"

Ellie froze in her tracks. Usually,

she loved being called a superstar. But not the way Marion had said it. That way sounded more like a bad word.

Ellie didn't know what to say. She felt her cheeks getting hot. She wasn't sure what from. Anger? Embarrassment? Ellie looked at Amy, who only looked at the ground.

Ellie opened her mouth. She wanted to say something back, but nothing came out. She closed it, turned, and stomped away.

During lunchtime rehearsal in the auditorium, Ellie was surrounded by her new friends from the play, but all she could think of was her old ones.

Suddenly, Ellie didn't feel like talking about the play.

Were Marion and Amy jealous of her? And what was up with Liz?

Chapter 8

An Ellie
Sometimes Forgets

Outside, after school, Ellie didn't wait for Marion or Amy, and Liz was nowhere to be seen.

Where is she? Ellie wondered, walking home alone. *How could she abandon me at a time like this?* Ellie wanted to ask Liz about Marion and Amy. After all, Ellie was the star of the play. She got to wear a glittery costume. She had lots of new friends. They must be jealous. Ellie was sure that's why Marion had said what she did.

When Ellie got home, she went to her room. Her Miss Ladybug costume was hanging on the closet door. *It really is so beautiful!* Ellie thought. *Maybe trying it on will cheer me up.*

For a couple of minutes it worked.

Ellie looked at herself in the mirror and smiled. She twirled and posed. She said some of her lines. She sang one of her songs. *This is what I'll look like up on stage!* she thought.

Then the feeling faded. Ellie remembered that awful way

Marion's voice sounded. She remembered the look on Amy's face. Quickly, she changed into her regular clothes. She flopped onto her bed. Suddenly, Ellie didn't feel excited about the play at all.

Just then the phone rang. Nana Gloria called up from downstairs: "Ellie! It's for you! It's Liz."

Finally! Ellie thought. *A friendly voice!* She flew down the stairs and ran to the phone. "Liz! Where have you been?" Ellie asked, out of breath. "I looked for you after school!"

Ellie waited for Liz to answer in

her usual easygoing way, but there was just silence at the other end.

"Liz? Liz!" Ellie said.

"I'm here, Ellie," Liz replied. Her voice was quiet and sounded . . .

different . . . like she wasn't smiling.

"Where were you at school today?" Ellie asked. She decided to skip to the important stuff. "You won't believe how mean Marion and Amy were to me today! They barely talked to me or looked at me. And then Marion called me 'superstar'! I think they are jealous of the whole play thing. I mean—"

"Ellie!" Liz shouted. Ellie stopped talking. "Did you forget anything today?" Liz asked her.

Forget anything? Ellie thought. She ran through things in her mind. She had her homework and reading book. She'd gone to play rehearsal. Oh! She still needed to try new hairstyles for the play. Plus she wanted to ask her mom if she could wear lipstick. . . .

"It's *Monday*!" said Liz, hinting.

"*Our* day? After school? At The Critter Club? You forgot to meet me at the barn after school, Ellie. I took care of everything all by myself!"

Ellie gasped. The bunnies! How had she forgotten?

She heard Liz sigh at the other

end. "This play—it's all you can think about!" Liz said. "It's bad enough that you forgot about the bunnies, but what about your best friend?"

Ellie felt a terrible sinking feeling in her stomach, but Liz wasn't done. "And in case you care, my painting won first place in the art contest. That's why the principal wanted to see me. It's going on to the state competition. You're not the only one who has exciting stuff happening, Ellie. Even if you've been acting like it!"

Liz hung up the phone before Ellie could answer. It was just as well, because, for once, Ellie didn't know what to say.

Chapter 9

A Secret Movie Star

Ellie felt a lump rising in her throat. She wanted to get out of the house. She didn't feel like telling her family why she was upset.

"I'm going for a bike ride!" she called into the kitchen.

"Okay!" Nana Gloria replied as the screen door slammed. In seconds, Ellie was riding away down the street.

At first she had no destination in mind. Then, suddenly, she wanted to visit the bunnies. She steered her bike toward Ms. Sullivan's place.

Ten minutes later Ellie was in the barn. Fluffy was in her lap. Frosty was sniffing her shoe. *Or is that one Floppy?* Ellie wondered. The third bunny was poking his head into her jacket pocket.

"I'm really sorry, bunnies," she

whispered to them. "I'm sorry I forgot you today." Tears welled up in her eyes. She couldn't hold it in. Ellie petted Fluffy as she cried and cried.

"Ellie?" came a voice at the door. Ellie turned. Ms. Sullivan was peeking into the barn.

"What's the matter?" She came over and wrapped an arm around Ellie. "Is everything okay?"

Ellie wiped her eyes on a sleeve. "Yes, Ms. Sullivan," she sniffed. "It's just—" The sobs came again and Ellie couldn't speak.

"Come on, dear," said Ms. Sullivan.

"Come in the house with me."

Ellie nodded. Together they put the bunnies back in the hutch. Then they walked across Ms. Sullivan's wide backyard and went in the back door of her gigantic gingerbread house.

As Ellie sat down in Ms. Sullivan's kitchen, Rufus came running in. He jumped up, resting his head and front paws on Ellie's knee. Ellie petted him while Ms. Sullivan got her some milk and cookies. By the time she set them on the table, Ellie had stopped crying.

Ellie explained about the play. She told Ms. Sullivan what Marion and Liz had said. She described the look on Amy's face.

"I guess I *have* been really focused on the play," said Ellie. "It just . . . it means a lot to me. Can't they see that?"

Ms. Sullivan smiled kindly. Then she got a twinkle in her eye. "Ellie, I have something to show you," she said. "Wait here a minute."

Ms. Sullivan left the room. Rufus stretched out under the table, waiting for cookie crumbs. When Ms. Sullivan returned, she had a photo in her hand. She handed it to Ellie.

Ruby Fairchild

Strangely,
the woman in the photo
looked familiar to Ellie, but where
had Ellie seen her before?

"As you know," said Ms. Sullivan.
"I haven't always lived in Santa
Vista. Before I moved here, I lived
in Hollywood."

Hollywood, California, thought Ellie, *where movies are made.* "Movies! That's it!" cried Ellie. "Have I seen this woman in a movie? In an older movie like the ones Nana Gloria likes to watch?"

Ms. Sullivan nodded. "Yes. That woman was a famous actress. Her screen name was Ruby Fairchild."

"Yeah! Ruby Fairchild!" said Ellie, looking again at the photo. "She was in *The Lost Sheep.* We watched it the other night!" Ellie looked up at Ms. Sullivan. "Why do you have her picture?" Ellie gasped.

"Did you *know* her in Hollywood?"

Ms. Sullivan laughed. "You could say that, Ellie," she said. "You see, Ruby Fairchild is . . . me!"

Ellie stared at Ms. Sullivan. Then she stared at the photo. "That's *you*!" she cried. "She *does* look like you!"

"Well, a much younger me," Ms. Sullivan said with a smile.

Ellie was amazed. She listened as Ms. Sullivan told her about her life in Hollywood. It sounded like Ellie's idea of heaven! The movie stars! The fancy parties! The awards! Signing autographs for crowds of cheering fans!

"I had a great career," said Ms. Sullivan, "but when I stopped making movies, I was ready for a quieter life. That's when I moved to Santa Vista." Ms. Sullivan sighed. "I thought if people here knew me as Ruby Fairchild, I'd never be left

alone. So I hid who I was and kept to myself. I didn't go out much, and I even lost touch with most of my old friends. A lot of days I was all alone in this giant house," she smiled, "until I got Rufus." She looked down at the big puppy under the table.

"Woof!" Rufus replied. His tail thumped against a chair leg.

"Then Rufus went missing, and you girls helped me find him," Ms. Sullivan went on. "Before The Critter Club, I hadn't made new friends in years!"

Ms. Sullivan put her arm around Ellie. "It's important to be kind to your friends. Keep them close. And here's a piece of advice, from one actress to another." Ellie grinned. Ruby Fairchild was calling *her* an actress? "Good friends will be there for you, but it can't *always* be about you."

Ellie finished her milk and cookies. Then Ms. Sullivan showed her more of her Hollywood stuff—old movie posters, scripts, and photos.

"Nana Gloria would flip to see all this!" Ellie said. "But don't you worry. Your secret will be safe with me, Ruby Fairchild—Ms. *Sullivan,* I mean."

Chapter 10

Making Things Right

Ellie rode home on her bike, thinking the whole way. She felt a lot better, thanks to Ms. Sullivan. She still dreamed of being a star, but she realized something important. Being a star would mean very little without friends.

"Dinner in fifteen minutes, Ellie!" Ellie's mom called as she came in the front door.

"Okay!" replied Ellie, running upstairs. She had just enough time. She needed to get some things down on paper.

In her room Ellie sat down at her desk. She took out three sheets of her special stationery. She chose a pretty red pen and began to write a note to Liz.

Ellie wrote a simi-lar note to Marion

Dear Liz,

You are right. I wanted to be the best Miss Ladybug I can be, but I forgot to be the best friend I can be. I promise to do better. I'm really, really, really sorry.

Your best friend (still, I hope!),
Ellie

and another to
Amy. She selected a special
sticker to seal each envelope. Next
she wrote her friends' names on the
front of each envelope.

Feeling hopeful, Ellie tucked the

notes into her backpack. Then she headed downstairs for dinner.

* * * * ❀ * * * * * * * * * * ♡ *

The next morning Ellie got to school a little early and left the notes on her friends' desks. Then she sat down at her own desk and took out a book.

Ellie pretended to read it, but

really she was peeking over the top. When Liz came in, Ellie watched her go to her desk. She saw the note and opened it. She was reading it!

Oh, what's she thinking? Ellie wondered.

She didn't have to wonder very long. Liz looked over

at Ellie. Slowly, a warm smile spread across Liz's face. Ellie smiled back.

Mrs. Sienna was starting class, but Ellie watched Marion and Amy read their notes, too. Amy smiled and gave Ellie a thumbs-up. Marion looked over and mouthed some words to Ellie.

"I'm sorry, too," she was saying.

Ellie nodded and smiled. She let out a happy sigh. It was like a weight had been lifted off of her.

The morning sped by. At

lunchtime Ellie met up with her friends in the hallway.

"Can you forgive me?" she asked them.

"Of course, Ellie!" said Liz. The girls wrapped Ellie in a big group hug.

"We're like sisters," said Amy.

Marion nodded. "Even sisters argue sometimes, but they always make up."

Ellie beamed. "Well, then, I have a favor to ask," she said. She looked at Liz. "Can I come over after school? I'd love to see your prizewinning painting. I'm so proud of you, Liz!"

"Oh yes!" cried Marion. "You

 have to see it! She got a blue first-place ribbon and everything!"

Liz laughed.

"Yes, of course. You can definitely come over and see it."

"I can't wait!" Ellie cried. "Oh! I almost forgot to tell you guys! I had an idea. It's about the bunnies. I think I know how to get people to adopt them!"

Bravo, Ellie!

The Santa Vista Elementary School auditorium was packed. It was Friday night—the night of the big play, *Miss Ladybug Saves Spring*.

The show sped by, number by number, and before long the play was almost over! Ellie and her cast mates had performed their roles perfectly. Now the red velvet curtain

opened one last time—for the big finale!

Flower dancers twirled around. Butterflies fluttered on tiptoe. Inchworms inched in time to the music. Dancing raindrops swung their legs up and down.

Last to come onstage was

Ellie—Miss Ladybug! She moved gracefully toward the front of the stage. The airy fabric of her sleeves fluttered behind her. There was something else behind her, too—a little red wagon. Miss Ladybug held its handle and pulled it along. Inside, munching on lettuce, were

three gray bunnies: Floppy, Fluffy, and Frosty!

From the audience came a great big "awwww."

Ellie slowly pulled the wagon across the stage. The audience read the sign on the wagon's side.

Then Ellie carefully handed the wagon to someone offstage.

The finale continued, building until the whole cast was onstage. They lined up in a row. One by one, each cast member took a bow. The crowd got to its feet, clapping and cheering.

As the lead, Ellie was the last to take her bow. The spotlight fell on her. She looked out into the audience. Everyone was there! She saw her mom and dad, Toby, and Nana Gloria, cheering. Behind them, Liz, Marion, and Amy waved at Ellie. Liz even whistled!

Then, from down in the first row, a figure approached the stage. It was Ms. Sullivan! She handed up

to Ellie a huge bouquet of red roses. "Bravo, Ellie!" she called out.

Ellie felt on top of the world. This was her moment. She had dreamed about it, but in her dreams, she had only seen herself.

The real moment was a million times better, and Ellie realized why. It was because her friends were there to share it with her.

the CRiTteR club

Liz Learns a Lesson

Table of Contents

Chapter 1   Hello, Summer!   249

Chapter 2   Change of Plans   263

Chapter 3   Liz's Secret   273

Chapter 4   Pop Quiz!   283

Chapter 5   Critter Sitters   293

Chapter 6   An Extra Student   303

Chapter 7   Counting Digits   319

Chapter 8   Day by Day   331

Chapter 9   The Final Grade   345

Chapter 10   The Best Day Ever   357

Hello, Summer!

Liz sat down on the bright green grass. She closed her eyes and soaked up the late-afternoon sunshine. "Can you believe it?" she said to her friends Ellie, Amy, and Marion. "Tomorrow is the *last day of school*!"

"Hel-lo, summer!" Ellie cried joyfully. "Hello, ice cream and

swimming and flip-flops—"

"And hello, lots of Critter Club!"
added Amy.

The Critter Club was an animal
rescue shelter the girls helped start.

Their friend Ms. Sullivan had come up with the idea after the girls found her lost puppy, Rufus. Amy's mom, a veterinarian, was a huge help too. Together they had turned Ms. Sullivan's big, empty barn into a cozy shelter for lost and lonely animals.

Thanks to The Critter Club, three abandoned bunnies had new homes. Right now the club had no animal guests . . . except for Rufus, of course!

That was about to change.

Marion opened her notebook.

Critter Club Pet Sitting		
Family	Pet	Name
Perez	Cat	Lentils
Hall	Dog	Ewok
Walker	3 Rabbits	Flppy, Flippy, + Steve
		Duke
Stein	Dog	Jose
Reed	Guinea Pig	Dax
Gray	Cat	Dr. Claw
Brooks	Cat	Spencer
Bruni	Dog	Mac + Izzy
Gonzalez	2 mice	Tootsie
Adams	Dog	

"We've already got ten families signed up for pet sitting!" she said.

Ellie let out a happy squeal. "Yay! Amy's mom was right. Pet sitting was such a great idea!"

"I think so too," said Amy. "While families are away on summer vacation, their pets can stay here!"

Liz flopped backward onto the soft, warm grass. She was *so* happy and excited. She'd get to spend lots of time with her friends, *and* she was done with homework until September!

Liz didn't mind school, but she sometimes had a hard time with school*work*—especially math. She would definitely not miss math over vacation.

The girls talked about their other summer plans. Marion was going to music day camp in July. She had been taking piano lessons since she was five.

Amy was going to help out at her mom's vet clinic. She also planned to spend a lot of weekends with her

dad in Orange Blossom. "He just got a new pool in his backyard!" Amy explained.

Ellie and her little brother, Toby, had fun plans with their grand-mother, Nana Gloria. "She's going to take us to the roller rink and the

zoo and the Santa Vista pool!" Ellie
said excitedly.

Liz sat up on the grass. "Well,
guess what I'm doing?" she said.

"Art?" asked Ellie, Marion, and
Amy at the same time. All four girls
started laughing.

"How did you guess?" Liz said

with a grin. Of course, her friends knew she loved to paint and draw. Mrs. Cummings's art room was Liz's favorite place at school. There, she never felt like the one who didn't "get it"—unlike when she was in math class.

"Okay, you're right!" Liz said. "Mrs. Cummings is teaching a class in June at the Santa Vista Library!" Liz glanced at Amy. "I'll look for you there?"

Amy giggled and nodded. "In the mystery section. I plan to read every Nancy Drew they've got. But first, I will see you all at school tomorrow . . . for our last day!"

The girls hopped onto their bikes and headed to their homes for dinner.

Liz took a deep, happy breath

as she pedaled. The warm air blew through her wavy blond hair.

Just one more day of school, she thought. *Then, let the summer begin!*

Chapter 2

Change of Plans

The last day of school is so fun! thought Liz.

She was on the playground, trying not to get tagged. Their teacher, Mrs. Sienna, had taken the class outside for an extra recess. Earlier, in their classroom, they had played Simon Says. Even the teachers were in the mood to have fun.

Back inside, Mrs. Sienna found a note on her desk. "Liz Jenkins," she said, "Mrs. Young would like to see you." Mrs. Young was the school principal.

"Me?" said Liz. "Oh . . . okay." She turned and headed for the main office. She felt a nervous flutter in her stomach. Had she done

something wrong? But Liz pushed the worry out of her mind. After all, what could go wrong on the last day of school?

Minutes later she was standing in the doorway of Mrs. Young's office.

"Hi, Liz," Mrs. Young said kindly.

Someone else was there too, with her back to Liz. She turned.

"Mom!" Liz sighed with relief. "Did I forget my lunch again?"

Mrs. Jenkins smiled at Liz. "No, honey," she said. "That's not why I'm here. Come have a seat." Her mom tapped the seat of the chair next to her. "Mrs. Young and I were just talking about math."

She handed Liz a yellow piece of paper.

MATH SUMMER SCHOOL!

Sharpen your skills over the summer.

When: Weekdays in June, 9:00 a.m. to noon

Where: Santa Vista Elementary School library

MATH? thought Liz. *In the summer?!* That sounded awful. Who would want to do *that*?

"Liz," said her mom, "we know you've had a hard time with math this year—even though you've tried your best. This class will give you a little extra help."

"But Mom," said Liz, "what about my art class?" She pointed to the flyer. "Both classes meet at the same time."

"I'm afraid you *need* to take this math class," Mrs. Young said. "You need it to keep up with the rest of the students."

269

Liz's mom put her arm around Liz. "I'm sorry, honey, but you're going to have to miss the art class with Mrs. Cummings."

Liz felt tears welling up in her eyes. Across the desk Mrs. Young suddenly looked blurry.

"The good news is that the math teacher, Mr. Brown, is very nice and funny," Mrs. Young said. "You'll have a blast. How does that sound?"

It sounded to Liz like she had no choice.

It sounded like the start of the worst summer ever.

271

Chapter 3

Liz's Secret

Liz tried to enjoy the rest of the day. It was hard. She couldn't stop thinking about summer school.

After school Ellie invited Liz, Amy, and Marion over to her house, but Liz just felt like going home. She wasn't ready to share her bad news. She felt so embarrassed.

I must just be the worst math

student in the whole grade, Liz thought to herself.

Liz told Ellie she wasn't feeling very well. "Oh, you poor thing," Ellie said. "You have to get better soon! After all it's the summer! There are so many things to do! And we have lots of plans!"

At home Liz's mom was waiting for her. She had made a batch of Liz's favorite organic cookies.

They sat down together at the

kitchen table, and Liz took a cookie. They talked more about summer school. "It probably won't help." Liz moped. "I just don't get math."

Her mom smiled. "When I was in college, there was this beautiful oak tree in the town park. After a storm it lost some big branches. The

town was going to cut it down. They said it was old and sick and too dangerous to have in the park."

Liz nodded and reached for another cookie. "So what happened?"

"Well, some friends and I called a tree specialist. We found out the tree *could* be healthy again with some special care. So we started a petition, and we got thousands of people to sign it," her mom said. "And guess what?"

"You saved the tree?" Liz guessed.

"We saved the tree!" her mom exclaimed, jumping out of her seat. Liz giggled. She loved how excited her mom got about nature.

Mrs. Jenkins sat down again. "Do you know why I told you that story, Liz?"

Liz pretended to think about it. "Does it have to do with math?"

Her mom nodded. "At first saving the tree seemed impossible. But each day we took tiny steps toward our goal—and we got there."

Liz felt better after talking to her mom. Dinner helped too. When her dad and her brother, Stewart, got home, her mom fired up the grill. Tofu dogs were, by far, Liz's

favorite summertime food.

After dinner Ellie stopped by. "I can't stay long," she told Liz. "I just wanted to see how you're feeling."

Liz smiled, thinking what a good friend Ellie was. "Actually, I *am* feeling better," she said.

She and Ellie sat down on the front steps. Liz told her about

summer school. "I was really upset about it before. That's what I meant about not feeling well."

Ellie linked arms with Liz. "Aw, I'm sorry, Liz," she said. "I know how excited you were about the class with Mrs. Cummings."

They sat for a minute, side by side, without saying anything. Crickets chirped loudly all around them.

"Look at it this way," Ellie said. "You still have afternoons at The Critter Club. And you'll have all of July and August when you're done!"

"That's true," said Liz with a

nod. "I will have that." She squeezed
Ellie's arm. "And I will have a great
friend like you, too."

Chapter 4

Pop Quiz!

Monday came too soon for Liz. It was the first day of summer school. At 8:55 a.m. she and her mom walked into the school lobby. It was strangely quiet.

Grrrrr, Liz grumbled silently. It felt like the *whole world* was on summer vacation. Her brother, Stewart, was still in bed!

In the library Liz's mom signed her in and they met Mr. Brown. He seemed nice enough to Liz, but she was distracted. She looked around the room. Was there anyone else here she knew?

There were about ten other kids, but Liz saw no familiar faces. *It's bad enough that I stink at math,* she thought. *Now all these other kids are going to find that out, too!*

Liz's mom said good-bye. "I'll

pick you up at noon," she told Liz. "Remember, day by day. Tiny steps."

Liz took an empty seat at a table. She shot a quick smile at the boy and girl already sitting there. They smiled back.

"Okay, everybody," Mr. Brown said. "Welcome to 'Melting Math.'" He laughed. "Get it? It's summertime? And math is cool? So the math is melting?"

Liz knew Mr. Brown was just trying to get everyone in a good mood, but she was still feeling grumpy. No one else laughed either.

"Never mind that," Mr. Brown continued cheerfully. "First things first." He passed out a sheet of paper to each of them. "Pop quiz!"

The class groaned.

What?! thought Liz. *A quiz? Already?*

Then Liz looked down at the quiz.

1) What is your name?

2) What is your favorite color?

3) What is your favorite ice-cream flavor?

4) If you weren't here, where would you be?

Okay, thought Liz. *Mr. Brown might be kind of fun, after all.*

After the quiz Mr. Brown passed out math problems. "Work with the others at your table," he said. "Then we'll go over the answers together."

Liz smiled again at the kids she was sitting with. "Hi," she said. "I'm

Liz. You guys don't go to school here, do you?"

The boy shook his head. "No," he said. "I go to Orange Blossom Elementary. My name is Robert." He smiled shyly.

"I'm Laura," said the girl. "I go to St. Mary's School."

They figured out that they were all the same age—eight! They also figured out that they would *all* rather be doing something else.

When Laura looked down at the worksheet, she frowned. "Oh no. Greater than, less than. I cannot keep those straight to save my life."

"Me neither," said Robert. "I'm also terrible at subtraction."

Liz smiled. Here were other kids with math struggles—just like her. She felt herself start to relax.

"And fractions!" Liz added.

"What is with fractions? How can three-eighths be *less* than one-half? Three is more than one and eight is more than two!"

Robert and Laura laughed at Liz's joke—not at Liz. Liz knew right then that the three of them were going to be friends.

The Critter Club

Book your summer pet sitting now.

Chapter 5

Critter Sitters

Liz told her mom all about class on the drive home. She could hardly wait to tell her friends, too.

At home Liz grabbed a sandwich before she hopped on her bike and headed for The Critter Club. Ellie, Amy, and Marion were all there organizing pet food and supplies.

When they saw Liz, they came

over and gave her a big group hug. "I guess everyone knows?" Liz asked. She looked at Ellie.

"I hope you don't mind!" Ellie said. "The girls were worried—wondering where you were."

Liz smiled. "I don't mind."

"Oh, okay," said Ellie. "Then tell us all about it! Don't leave anything out!"

"Ellie, give her a break," Amy teased her friend.

"No, it's okay," Liz said. "I was nervous this morning, but it wasn't so bad."

The girls sat down in a circle, each on an upside-down bucket.

"Is school really empty and quiet?" Ellie wanted to know.

"Do you know anyone in class?" Amy asked.

"And what's the teacher like?" Marion questioned.

Liz told them all about it—about Mr. Brown, the fun pop quiz, and Robert and Laura. "There's going to be a test every Friday." Liz looked around the barn. "So what did I miss?" she asked her friends.

Ellie, Amy, and Marion looked at each other. They shared a secret

smile. "Should we show her now?" Ellie asked.

"What?" asked Liz. "Show me what?"

They led her over to a glass tank on a side table. "The Kim family dropped off their pet this morning,"

said Amy. "They're going on a four-week cruise. So we're going to watch Herman."

"Um, no," said Ellie. "*Liz* is going to watch Herman. *I* am not watching Herman."

Liz looked in the tank. Sitting on one of the rocks was a big fuzzy tarantula!

"He is so adorable!" cooed Liz. She put her face close to the glass. "Hi, Herman!"

Of all the girls Liz was the one most into . . . *unusual* pets. She had a pet ferret named Reggie, whom she adored. As Liz liked to say, all pets needed love: mice, salamanders, snakes, Madagascar hissing cockroaches. . . .

Liz grinned through the glass at the spider. "Herman," she said. "This summer is looking up!"

301

Chapter 6

An Extra Student

The next morning Liz rode her bike to school. Laura was at the bike rack.

"Hi, Liz!" Laura said as she parked her own bike.

"Hi, Laura!" Liz replied. "You live close enough to bike too?"

Laura nodded. "Yep. I live about three blocks away. Over by the public library."

Liz felt a pang of sadness. She wished she were at the public library right now, at Mrs. Cummings's art class, instead of in her school's library.

Just then a car pulled up in the drop-off circle. Robert hopped out.

"Hi!" he said, walking over to Liz and Laura. "What did you guys think of the homework?"

Liz groaned. "Ugh!" she said. The three of them headed for the school entrance. "Regrouping is another thing I'm terrible at."

"Me too," said Robert.

"Me three," said Laura. Suddenly she stopped in her tracks. "Hey, that's a crazy-looking rock," she said, pointing at the ground.

Liz and Robert stopped too. There was a brownish green rock right on the sidewalk. It had some kind of pattern on it. "Oh, wow," said Robert. "*Is* it a rock? Or is it a . . . ?"

Slowly, a little head peeked out from under the rock. Then four little legs appeared. The rock started to move!

"It's a turtle!" Liz exclaimed happily. "Cool!"

Moving carefully, the three of them knelt by the turtle's side. "He's so beautiful," Liz said.

"Where do you think he came from?" Robert asked.

Liz looked around. "I think there's a little pond back there," she said. She pointed toward the woods next to the school. "Maybe he lives there."

"Maybe he's someone's pet?" Laura suggested.

They stood watching the turtle walk in slow motion. He was inching— very, very slowly— toward the street.

"I don't think we should leave

him here," Liz said. "What if he crawls into the road?"

They had to get to class. Liz made a quick decision. She emptied her backpack. She gently picked up the turtle and placed him carefully at the bottom. Then she zipped the bag back up, but not all the way.

"Come on," she said, picking up her homework sheets. "Let's get to class!"

Robert and Laura looked at each other, their eyes wide. Robert shrugged. Laura giggled. Liz smiled, a twinkle in her eye.

Then, together, they hurried to class.

• • • ◌ • • • • • • • • • • • ♥ • • • •

Mr. Brown began class by writing some addition problems on the whiteboard.

Under the table Liz's backpack wiggled. *I hope he has enough air in there*, Liz thought.

"Okay!" Mr. Brown said. "So, for which problems will you need to regroup?" He called on a girl at another table.

While she answered, Liz peeked under the table.

Is it too dry for him in there?, Liz wondered.

"Great!" Mr. Brown was saying to the girl. "Who else? Are there any other problems here that will need regrouping?" He called on Robert.

Maybe I should take the turtle to the bathroom, Liz thought. *He could swim in the sink.*

"Good, Robert," Mr. Brown said.

$$\begin{array}{r} 72 \\ +19 \\ \hline \end{array} \quad \begin{array}{r} 46 \\ +27 \\ \hline \end{array} \quad \begin{array}{r} 14 \\ +3 \\ \hline \end{array}$$

"Now there's just one left. One more problem on the board that will need regrouping. Who can tell me which . . . ?"

What if he's hungry? Liz was thinking. *But what do turtles eat, anyway?*

"Liz?" Mr. Brown called. "Liz, can you tell me?"

Startled, Liz jumped a little in her seat. "Oh! Uh . . ." She hadn't heard the question. What should she say? She shifted in her seat. Her right leg bumped

her backpack under the table. It fell over.

Liz squealed loudly, then blurted out: *"Turtle!"*

She reached down and propped the backpack up. When she sat up again, everyone was staring at her.

Liz flashed a smile. She tried to act natural, but she could feel her cheeks blush.

"Liz, do you have something to share with the class?" Mr. Brown asked.

She looked across the table at Robert and Laura. They were both trying to contain their laughter.

Then Liz picked up her backpack and stood up. She walked over to Mr. Brown's desk. She reached inside her backpack and pulled out the turtle.

The whole class gasped, and the turtle slowly pulled its head into its shell.

What would Mr. Brown say?

"See, he was outside on the sidewalk," Liz explained. "It looked like he was headed into the street. I didn't want to leave him. . . ."

Mr. Brown's eyes were wide. He looked surprised, but was he mad? For a moment Liz couldn't tell . . . until his mouth turned up at the corners. He was smiling! Then he was laughing!

"Well, this is a first," he said. "I've never had a reptile in class before!"

Chapter 7

Counting Digits

Liz breathed a sigh of relief. She was glad she wasn't in trouble.

"I bet we can find him a cozier spot," Mr. Brown said. He spotted the librarian's empty fish tank. He let Laura and some others go outside to find some rocks. Meanwhile, Mr. Brown took Liz and Robert with him to get water.

"Make it *warm* water," Robert told Mr. Brown. "My dad once had a turtle and they like it warm."

"Oh! And I can find out what turtles like to eat," said Liz. "I'll bring food for him tomorrow."

Before long, the tank was the perfect turtle home.

"Our new friend looks very happy," said Mr. Brown.

"Now let's get back to math."

"*Awww!*" everyone moaned.

But Mr. Brown had some fun up his sleeve. "We're going to use math to name our turtle friend."

"Hooray!" the class cheered.

Mr. Brown laughed. "See? Math

can be fun!" Together they made a list of some math-themed names. Mr. Brown wrote them all on the whiteboard.

Then the class voted. Each person put a tally mark next to their favorite.

"Well, it looks like our turtle

has a name," said Mr. Brown. "Welcome, Digit!"

As the first week of class went on, everyone seemed excited to have a class pet—even Mr. Brown.

On Wednesday they worked on greater than and less than. Liz's favorite problem was:

Which is greater :
a million turtles or
a billion turtles?

On Thursday they did word problems. Some were really tricky.

Digit crawls two inches on Sunday, ten inches on Monday, and twelve inches on Tuesday. How many feet does Digit crawl all together?

Liz added the numbers: 2 + 10 + 12. She wrote down her answer: twenty-four. She raised her hand.

"Before I call on anyone, here's a hint," said Mr. Brown. "The first step in solving a word problem is not getting the *answer*. It's getting the *question*."

Huh? thought Liz. She reread the problem. This time she noticed: How many *feet* does Digit crawl all

together? She erased her 24. Twenty-four inches was the same as . . .

Mr. Brown called on her. "Two feet!" Liz said.

"Excellent, Liz!" Mr. Brown said.

Finally it was Friday—test day. Mr. Brown went over everything they had covered that week. Then he passed out the test papers.

Liz took a deep breath. She had stayed home from The Critter Club on Thursday afternoon so she could study hard. She'd asked Ellie to tell Amy and Marion why. Then, after dinner that evening, Ellie had called on the phone. "Everybody says, 'Good luck!' You're going to do great!"

Liz picked up her pencil. "I hope Ellie's right," she whispered to herself.

The library was silent for the rest of the class. Liz worked hard and lost track of time.

After class Liz walked out into the sunshine. Laura was right behind her. "So, what did you think?" she asked Liz.

"You know," said Liz, "it wasn't *too* bad."

Actually, for the first time ever, Liz felt like she wasn't totally awful at math.

Chapter 8

Day by Day

The weeks started to fly by. In the mornings Liz went to class. She saw Laura and Robert. She checked on Digit. She tried hard in math, and it was paying off! On her first three tests, Liz got most of the questions right!

Every day, after stopping home for lunch, she went to The Critter

Club. Sometimes all four of the girls were there. Other times it was just two or three of them. Their June schedule was hanging in the barn.

JUNE

Sun	Mon	Tue	Wed	Thu	Fri	Sat
						1 Marion HorseShow
2	3 Ellie w/ Nana Gloria Marion Piano Lesson	4 Amy working at vet clinic	5 Marion Piano Lesson	6 Amy working at vet clinic	7 Ellie w/ Nana Gloria	8
9 Amy day at Dad's	10 Marion Piano Lesson	11 Amy working at vet clinic	12 Ellie w/ Nana Gloria Marion Piano Lesson	13 Amy working at vet clinic	14 Ellie w/ Nana Gloria	15
16 Ellie w/ Nana Gloria	17 Marion Piano Lesson	18 Ellie w/ Nana Gloria Amy working at vet clinic	19 Marion Piano Lesson	20 Amy working at vet clinic	21	22 Marion Horse Show
23 Amy day at Dad's	24 Marion Piano Lesson	25 Amy working at vet clinic	26 Marion Piano Lesson	27 Amy working at vet clinic	28 Ellie w/ Nana Gloria	29
30						

Of course Liz had told Robert and Laura all about The Critter Club. On a few afternoons they came to help out too. They both loved animals. Plus, it was great to have the extra help. For part of

June the club was superbusy. They were pet sitting for four dogs, three cats, some mice, a guinea pig, three rabbits—and Herman the tarantula. It took a lot of work to keep them all happy!

At dinnertime Liz rode her bike home. Her route took her right past the Santa Vista Library. Liz still felt sad about missing her art class, but she just tried not to think about it too much.

Day after day, week after week, Liz worked hard.

On the last Wednesday evening in June, Liz was in her room. She was working on a homework sheet when she suddenly realized something.

The last test is . . . tomorrow!

It had slipped Liz's mind until now. Usually *Friday* was test day, but this was the final week of class. Mr. Brown had said that their test would be on *Thursday*. He would hand them back on Friday, the last day of class!

Liz felt a little panicked. *Can I*

do it? she wondered. *What if I completely mess this one up?* She dug around in her backpack for her practice sheets. "I have to go over everything from this week!" she told her ferret, Reggie.

Just then Liz's brother, Stewart, popped into her room. Stewart was twelve years old. The two of them got along okay, but lately Stewart had been teasing her about math.

He thought he was so smart, just because he was in sixth grade.

"Hey, Lizzie," he said.

"Not now, Stewart!" Liz snapped at him. "I don't have time to be made fun of! Tomorrow's my last math test."

"Who? *Me?*" Stewart said. "I wasn't going to tease you."

Liz squinted at him. Was he telling the truth?

"Hey, how's that turtle you found?" Stewart asked.

"Digit?" said Liz. "He's good. He's eating a lot!"

Stewart nodded. "Well, I think it's cool that you saved him. Turtles

are awesome! They just do their own thing. They can't be rushed. 'Slow and steady wins the race,' and all that." Stewart turned to go, then stopped. "Hey, that's a good tip for the test, right?"

Liz watched Stewart go. Her brother sometimes said crazy stuff. *But this time*, thought Liz, *he kind of makes sense.*

• • •◦ • • • • • • • • •◦ • • •

The next morning Liz got to school a few minutes early. She was ready to go!

She stopped by Digit's tank.

"Don't tell Stewart," she whispered,
"but I'm going to take his advice.
Slow and steady wins the race.
Right, Digit?"

Robert came in, then Laura. They both gave Liz a thumbs-up.

Mr. Brown spent most of the class doing a big review. Then he passed out the test papers.

Liz took a deep breath. *Stay calm,* she told herself. *Don't rush. Check your work. You'll be fine.* Liz picked up her pencil, and she began.

For the rest of the class the only sound came from pencils scratching on papers. Liz finished just as Mr. Brown stood up. "Pencils down," he said. He collected the papers. "See you all tomorrow! I'll pass back your graded tests then."

Liz could hardly wait until tomorrow's class!

Chapter 9

The Final Grade

Liz had that fluttery feeling in her stomach again. It was the last day of summer school, and Mr. Brown was about to pass back the tests.

Liz could hardly sit still. She couldn't stand not knowing how she'd done! She had been thinking about it since she finished the test the day before. At The Critter Club

afterward, her friends had been so happy for her.

"You've worked really hard and done your best," Marion had said.

Even Ms. Sullivan and Rufus had dropped by the barn. "I'm very proud of you, Liz," Ms. Sullivan said. Rufus jumped up on Liz and licked her cheek.

"Rufus is proud of you too!" Amy joked.

Now, sitting in the library, Liz wondered: What would she tell them if she *hadn't* passed?

"Okay!" said Mr. Brown. "Before

Last Day!

I return the tests, I just want to say something. . . ."

Liz's palms were sweating. She couldn't wait another moment!

"I am so proud of this class," Mr. Brown went on. "You worked very, very hard all month long."

He gave a huge smile. "Oh! And there's one more thing . . . you all passed! Congratulations!"

"Hooray!" the class cheered. Liz jumped up out of her seat. Laura and Robert jumped up too.

"Great job, Liz," Mr. Brown said. He held out her test. She took it and

looked at the grade at the top. It was an A!

I got an A? she thought. *In MATH?* "Yahoo!" Liz cried. She could not wait to show her mom and dad—and Stewart, too!

Robert and Laura also did well! Everyone was so excited!

And just like that summer school was over! Kids gathered their things and headed for the door. Laura and Robert got up to leave.

"Hey," said Liz, "maybe we could meet up later at The Critter Club?"

"I'll ask my mom!" Laura said.

"Me too!" said Robert. "Gotta run. My mom's going to flip when she sees my test!"

Laura and Robert headed out, but Liz hung back. She walked up to Mr. Brown. "Good-bye, Mr. Brown," she said. "And thanks a lot. You know, you actually made math pretty fun."

"Thanks, Liz!" Mr. Brown said. "And you know what else? You're much better at math than you think you are."

Liz beamed. *"Really?"* she said.

Mr. Brown nodded. "Yep! It's okay if it takes you longer than others. It doesn't mean you can't get there." He looked over at Digit's tank. "Right, Digit?"

Then he said, "Oh! Speaking of Digit . . . I'm going on vacation in a few days. Do you think Digit could go home with you? Would your parents mind?"

A smile spread across Liz's face. "Don't worry, Mr. Brown," she said. "I know a place where Digit will be well taken care of."

The Critter Club had just gotten one more guest.

Chapter 10

The Best Day Ever

At home Liz's mom took one look at her test and gave Liz a big hug. "I am *so* proud of you, honey! This calls for a celebration!"

Liz's mom picked up the phone. She called Robert's parents and Laura's parents. She asked if the kids could come out for lunch.

An hour later Liz and her

mom picked them both up. The four of them went to Liz's favorite restaurant.

Digit came along too. Liz gave him some turtle food pellets so they could all eat together.

After lunch Liz's mom dropped

them off at The Critter Club. They were excited to show Digit around.

Laura and Robert hopped out of the car. As Liz carried Digit's tank out, she said, "Thanks, Mom! See you later at home."

"Oh, Liz! Wait!" her mom called. "I was so excited about your test, I almost forgot to tell you!"

"Tell me what?" Liz asked.

"I saw Mrs. Cummings at the grocery store," Liz's mom said. "She's teaching another art class at the library in July. How does that sound?" Her mom was smiling.

Liz's mouth fell open. She had to put Digit down. She didn't want to drop him while she jumped up and down for joy!

Liz threw her head back and shouted, "This *is* going to be the best summer after all!"

the CRitteR club

Marion Takes a Break

Table of Contents

Chapter 1   Too Much to Do   367

Chapter 2   Marion Makes a Mess   379

Chapter 3   One Wrong Step   389

Chapter 4   Friends to the Rescue!   401

Chapter 5   Back to School?   413

Chapter 6   Broken Dreams   421

Chapter 7   The Plan   429

Chapter 8   The Sixth Kitten   439

Chapter 9   Kittens and Cookies   451

Chapter 10   Surprise!   465

Too Much to Do

In the school cafeteria Marion saw Amy, Ellie, and Liz sitting near the window. Marion hurried over. She hoped she would have time to eat her lunch. The recess bell was going to ring in just ten minutes!

"What took you so long?" Amy asked. She scooted down the bench to make space for Marion.

"I couldn't find my lunch!" Marion said, sitting down. "I thought it was in my cubby, but it was actually in my backpack under my ballet shoes and leotard."

I've got to get organized! Marion thought as she started to eat. *Better add that to my to-do list!*

Marion was good at making lists. It helped to keep her busy life in order. Now that it was fall, Marion was busier than ever! She worked very hard in school and always got perfect grades. She also had piano lessons and ballet class every week.

Then there was her horse, Coco. Marion went to the stables at least three times a week. Having a horse was a lot of work, but Marion loved every bit of it.

"So what were you talking about?" Marion asked. She took a big bite of her sandwich.

"The kittens!" Ellie exclaimed. There was a new litter of kittens at The Critter Club, the animal shelter that the four girls helped run in their friend Ms. Sullivan's barn. The girls had met Ms. Sullivan when they found her lost puppy, Rufus.

After that, Ms. Sullivan decided

the town needed an animal shelter. She had an empty barn; Amy's mom, Dr. Purvis, had a lot of advice to offer since she was a veterinarian; and the girls had lots of energy— plus a love of animals.

So The Critter Club began! Since then the girls had helped bunnies and a turtle. They had even done pet sitting over the summer. Now it was up to them to find homes for an entire litter of kittens!

The kittens' mother was a stray cat. When a teacher found them all behind the school, she brought them to the vet clinic. Dr. Purvis had suggested that the five healthy kittens stay at The

Critter Club, and the girls were very excited to help take care of them!

"The mother cat and one kitten are still at the clinic," Amy told her friends. "My mom said that the mama cat needs more rest. And even though the tabby kitten's injured paw is getting better, he still needs to heal for a while longer too."

The girls took turns helping out at The Critter Club after school and on weekends. "Liz and I had such a great time at the club yesterday afternoon. Those kittens are just so cute!" Ellie squealed.

"That's the thing," Amy said, "it should be easy to find homes for them. I was thinking . . . what if we have a big party at The Critter Club? People could come meet the kittens!"

Marion, Ellie, and Liz all nodded. "That's a great idea!" said

Liz. "Everyone would see how cute they are!"

"We could have music!" Ellie suggested. She loved to perform. "I could sing!"

"We could get dressed up!" Marion added. She had a silver dress that would be perfect.

"We could put up pretty lights—and some artwork!" said Liz. She was an amazing artist.

Marion imagined how wonderful Liz's paintings would look hanging around The Critter Club. They would really jazz up the barn!

Just then the recess bell rang. Marion chewed fast, trying to finish her sandwich. Then the four friends headed outside. It was autumn in Santa Vista, but in their part of California, it never got too cold.

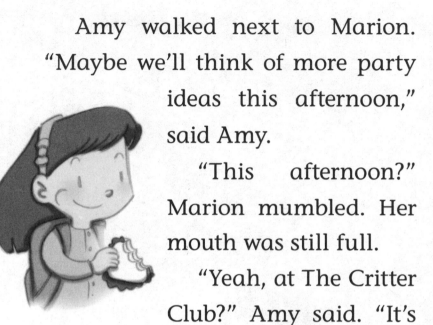

Amy walked next to Marion. "Maybe we'll think of more party ideas this afternoon," said Amy.

"This afternoon?" Marion mumbled. Her mouth was still full.

"Yeah, at The Critter Club?" Amy said. "It's Monday—our day to help out. Remember?"

Marion had forgotten! It wasn't like her to get her schedule mixed up. "Uh? The Critter Club? Of course I will be there!"

Chapter 2

Marion Makes a Mess

If we finish early, I'll have time to ride Coco before dinner, Marion was thinking.

"Marion, I think you fed that kitten already," Amy was saying.

Marion looked down. The light gray kitten wasn't drinking. He didn't seem interested in Marion's bottle of milk. "Oh! You're right!"

Marion exclaimed. "What am I doing?"

She and Amy were at The Critter Club, feeding the tiny kittens.

Dr. Purvis had told them that the kittens were only about five weeks old! Feeding such young cats was tricky. Luckily, Dr. Purvis had shown the girls just what to do. She had even made them a poster to remind them of the steps.

How to Feed the Kittens ♡

Step 1: Take out one container marked "Kitten Milk" from the refrigerator. This is special milk that is just like their mother's.

Step 2: Pour the milk into a clean baby bottle.

Step 3: Warm the bottle in the bottle warmer until light turns green.

Step 4: Hold kitten, sitting up, in your lap, or let kitten lie on his/her belly while eating. Do not cradle kitten belly up like a baby.

381

Marion and Amy had come to the club right after school. Marion had been rushing around ever since. She really wanted to get to the stables to ride Coco. They had a big competition coming up. Marion and Coco had won it last year, and

Marion had her sights on taking the blue ribbon again this year. There was a good reason blue was her favorite color!

The only thing was, they would need some extra practice if they wanted to win.

Marion warmed a bottle for the black kitten. But hurrying across the barn, she dropped it on the barn floor and had to make up a new one. Then she knocked over the bottle warmer, spilling the water inside. Next, Marion didn't screw a bottle top on tight enough. Some milk spilled on the white kitten.

"Oh, for goodness' sake!" she cried. "I just can't do anything right!"

Amy came over. "Marion, are you okay?" Amy asked kindly. "You don't seem like yourself."

She's right, thought Marion. *I'm not myself. I never, ever mess up this*

much! Marion was used to getting things right the first time.

She sighed and wiped up the milk. "I'm fine," she said. "Just in a rush!" She looked up at Amy. "I need to get to the stables before dinner. We have a competition coming up,

and Coco and I need some extra practice."

Amy smiled. "Oh, I get it now," she said. "Well, I can finish up here if you need to go."

Marion studied Amy's face. "Really?" Marion asked. "Are you sure?"

Amy looked around. "We're almost done anyway," she said. "Really! You should go. Say hi to Coco for me!"

Marion felt so lucky to have such a great best friend. She gave Amy a huge hug. "Thank you!" she said as she turned to go. "You are the best!"

chapter 3

One Wrong Step

That afternoon Marion rode Coco until the sun started to set.

The next day, Tuesday, she headed to the stables right after school. She and Coco worked on walk, trot, canter, and gallop all afternoon.

Then on Wednesday afternoon Marion had her riding lesson. She and her teacher worked on some low jumps.

By Thursday Marion was starting to feel ready. "We've got two more weeks, Coco," she said to her pretty brown horse. Marion was brushing Coco in her stall. "Two weeks until the show. I know we can do it."

She looked over at the stall door. Coco's

ribbons hung in a row. "We'll get you another blue ribbon to hang up!"

Marion said good-bye to Coco before heading to the changing room. She *loved* her riding outfit—her tall boots, her breeches, her crisp, navy blue jacket, but Marion also loved what she'd worn to school that day. It was her *favorite fall outfit*: her corduroy skirt, lavender cardigan, purple tights, and purple flats. She was excited to put them back on!

"Marion!" a voice called from outside her dressing cubby. "Are you there?" Marion knew that voice. It was her six-year-old sister, Gabby. She took riding lessons at the stable too. Gabby was going to compete in the junior division at the horse show. "Come on! Mom and I are waiting in the car!"

"Uh, I'm coming!" Marion called. She hurried to pull on

her tights, but pulling on tights fast was very hard to do. Marion stepped into her flats and hurried outside. She saw her mom's car by the corral fence. Marion ran across the stable yard.

Halfway there she stepped in a dip in the gravel path. Her left foot twisted in a strange way when she landed.

"Ow!" Marion cried. She felt a sharp pain in her ankle. Her leg gave out and she fell onto the gravel. "Ow! My ankle!" It felt so weird—and hurt *so much*!

When Marion didn't get up, Marion's mom and sister ran over from the car.

What happened next was a big blur. Marion's mom and sister helped her up, but she couldn't walk. Standing on her ankle hurt

way too much so Marion's mom gave her a piggyback ride to the car. They drove straight to the hospital, where Marion's dad, a doctor, met them in the emergency room.

Dr. Ballard examined her ankle and ordered an X-ray. Marion began to worry.

Before long, Marion's dad put

his hand on her shoulder. He held the X-ray up to the light.

"Bad news, kiddo. It looks like you have a pretty bad sprain," he said. "You're going to need a cast."

"A *cast*?" Marion was shocked. "For how long?"

"At least three weeks—maybe four," her dad said. "You'll have crutches to help you get around, but you will need to take it easy for a while. But guess what? Casts come in all kinds of cool colors!"

For once Marion didn't care about fashion. She couldn't believe

397

what she was hearing. This *wasn't* happening! "No, no, no! I can't be in a cast for three weeks! Dad, the horse show is in *two weeks*!"

Her dad put down the X-ray. He

took Marion's hand. "I'm really sorry, honey," he said. "It's going to take time for your ankle to heal." He sighed a big sigh. "I'm afraid the horse show is out."

Chapter 4

Friends to the Rescue!

Marion closed her book and tossed it onto the sofa. She just *couldn't* concentrate.

It was Friday afternoon. She'd had the cast less than twenty-four hours, and already she was tired of it. She had missed school because she wasn't used to walking with the crutches yet.

"By Monday you'll be a pro," her dad had said that morning. "Then you can try them at school."

Monday couldn't come soon enough for Marion. *I'm missing everything!* she thought. *I can't go to ballet next week. I can't ride Coco. I don't even know what's going on in math class!*

Marion's mom was home with her, so Marion's dad picked up Gabby from her riding lesson at the stables. She walked in with her riding clothes still on. Marion

couldn't help feeling envious.

What's worse than not being able to ride in the horse show? she asked herself. *Having a sister who is riding in the horse show.* Marion knew it wasn't her sister's fault. Still, it was going to be *so* hard to watch Gabby ride when Marion couldn't.

Just then the doorbell rang. Marion heard her mom open the front door. Moments later Amy, Ellie, and Liz poked their heads in to the family room. "Can we come in?" Amy asked.

"*Yes!*" Marion cried. She was so glad to see her friends.

Ellie handed Marion a very pretty bouquet of flowers. "At school Mrs. Sienna told the class about your ankle!" Ellie said.

"We had to come see you," added Liz. She gave Marion a get-well card she had made.

"We thought you might need cheering up," said Amy. "Oh, and these." She handed Marion a tin. Marion opened the lid. Inside were Amy's mother's famous oatmeal raisin cookies. They were Marion's favorite.

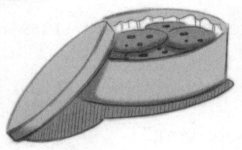

Marion forced a smile. "Thanks, guys," she said. She put the flowers, the card, and the cookies next to her on the coffee table.

"Wait," said Amy. "Aren't you going to have a cookie?"

Marion shrugged. "Not right now," she said with a big sigh. "I'm not hungry."

Amy looked at Ellie and Liz. "Uh-oh," Amy said. "Not hungry for her favorite cookies? She *does* need to be cheered up."

Ellie giggled. "Well, then, let's tell her," she said. "Listen, Marion. About the sleepover tonight—"

Marion slapped her forehead as it hit her. "The sleepover!" she cried. "Today is Friday! I forgot!"

The four girls had a sleepover almost every Friday night. They each took turns hosting. Marion knew that this week it was at Liz's house.

"Oh," she groaned, "*another thing I can't do!*" She wasn't feeling up to getting off the sofa—not until she could practice more with her crutches.

"Yeah," said Amy. "We thought you might not be able to come to Liz's."

"So we brought the sleepover to you!" said Liz.

Marion gasped. "Really?" she said. "You mean we can have it here instead?"

"Sure!" Liz said. "I'll host next week instead. Now, you've got to let me sign your cast!"

"Ooh! Me too!" said Amy.

"Me three!" said Ellie.

"Sure!" Marion said. Then she smiled—for real this time.

chapter 5

Back to School?

On Monday morning Marion woke up feeling excited. After practicing with her crutches all weekend, her mom and dad had agreed she could go back to school!

Marion hopped on her good foot to her closet. She wanted to pick out the perfect outfit.

Then she realized something.

She couldn't wear tights or leggings. They wouldn't fit over her cast. And—Marion gasped—she could only wear one shoe!

None of my favorite outfits will look as good with this cast! she thought.

Marion had to wear her least favorite jeans. And for her one shoe, her mom wanted her to wear a sneaker. "Comfort and grip. That's what you need!" Mrs. Ballard said.

Marion checked her outfit in the mirror. "This day is not off to a good start," she said grumpily.

At school things didn't get much better. It took her forever to get from the drop-off circle to her classroom. She was the last one in her seat. Marion hated being last.

In gym class Marion couldn't play kickball. She had to sit on the bench and watch. Amy, Liz, and Ellie took turns keeping her company.

At lunchtime Marion couldn't carry her lunchbox *and* walk on crutches at the same time. Amy was happy to carry her lunch for her, but Marion didn't like the feeling of not being able to do things on her own.

As the week went on, Marion got more frustrated. At her piano lesson her cast made it hard to use the foot pedal. None of Marion's songs sounded right.

At ballet class, all the students were learning new moves. Marion went so she could at least see the steps. But she couldn't practice them. *Wow, everyone looks so graceful*, she thought. She wished she were up there, right in front.

Hardest of all was visiting Coco. The stables were very busy with riders getting ready for the horse show.

Marion fed Coco a carrot and brushed her mane. "I'm so sorry, Coco," she whispered. "You have worked so hard to win. I'm just a huge failure—at everything."

419

Broken Dreams

Finally it was Thursday—Marion's and Amy's turn after school at The Critter Club. *At last!* thought Marion. *Feeding the little kittens is something fun that even I can do with this cast!*

It turned out this wasn't exactly true. Marion couldn't get around on crutches while holding a kitten in her arms. And she definitely couldn't get around with a kitten *and* a bottle.

"That's okay," said Amy. "We'll feed them together. You hold this one. I'll get the bottle."

That's when Marion's frustration bubbled over. "I can't do anything right!" she burst out. Tears rolled down her cheeks. "I took one wrong step, and now my ankle is sprained! This cast will be on for weeks. And everything keeps on going without me! I'll never be able to catch up!"

She covered her face with her hands and sobbed. Amy hugged her tight.

"Oh, Marion, it's okay! You're going to be better so soon!" Amy said. "You make it sound like

everything is a big race, but it isn't. You don't have to be number one all the time."

Amy let go of Marion. She looked her right in the eye. "You know, we all love you for *you*," Amy said. "It's not because you get awesome grades, or

play piano amazingly . . . or dance like a pro . . . or win blue ribbons with Coco. Should I keep going?"

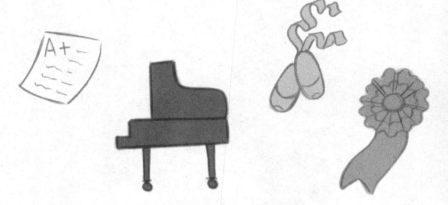

Marion laughed through her tears. "No, that's okay," she said.

Amy smiled. "It must be really hard not to be able to do your favorite things, but maybe, for now, just think of the things you *can* do."

Amy looked down at the kittens. "Like feed these fuzz balls."

Marion wiped her tears. She took a deep breath. "You're right," she said with a smile. "Thanks, Amy."

Then, the girls fed the kittens— together.

Chapter 7

The Plan

The next day at school Amy had great news.

"Mom says the kitten with the injured paw is doing much better!" she told the girls at lunch. "He can go home—well, he could if he had a home."

"Yeah," said Liz. "Too bad none of the kittens have been adopted.

Hey! He could come stay at The Critter Club too, right?"

"Great idea, Liz!" Ellie said.

Amy nodded. "He might need some special care for a little while, but we can handle that. Right?"

"Right!" the others chimed in.

"And while he gets stronger," said Marion, "we can work on finding homes for *all* the kittens!"

Marion was feeling more like

her old self again. Her talk with
Amy had helped a lot. She got out
a notebook and pen to start a to-do
list.

"So what about Amy's idea?"
Marion asked. "Having a big party
at The Critter Club so people can
meet the kittens?"

"I still love that idea," said Ellie.

"There's just one thing," said Liz. "Throwing a big party costs money. We'd have to buy food and decorations."

"That's true," Amy agreed. "It could get pretty expensive."

Marion thought it over. How could they get lots of people to meet the kittens? She remembered when they were trying to find homes for

some bunnies. Ellie was starring in the school play. She had gotten the bunnies up on stage.

Could we get the kittens in some kind of show? thought Marion. *A show . . . A show . . .* Then it hit her. *The horse show!*

"I've got it!" Marion exclaimed. "We could bring the kittens to the big horse show next weekend! We

could set up a booth. There will be lots of kids and parents there!"

"Yes!" said Amy. "Marion, that's a *great* idea. Maybe my mom could bake some cookies for us to give away to people so they stop by the booth!"

"I could bring my karaoke machine!" Ellie chimed in.

"Ellie," began Liz, "you are a *fantastic* singer, but—"

"Oh no!" Ellie said. "Not so I can sing. We

could use the microphone to get people's attention."

Liz giggled. "Oh! That makes sense. And I can be in charge of decorating the booth."

Suddenly Marion knew what *she* wanted to be in charge of. "Can I make a special collar for each kitten?" she asked. "That way they'll each look their best for the big day."

The girls agreed it was a plan—a *great* plan!

437

Chapter 8

The Sixth Kitten

Marion lined up the kittens' collars she had made so far. "Five down, one to go!" she said.

She was at The Critter Club with Amy, Ellie, and Liz. All four had been spending extra time there. The horse show was only three days away, and there was a lot they wanted to get organized.

"Wow, Marion! Those are all so pretty!" Ellie said.

"Thanks!" Marion replied. She had worked hard on her creations. She had thought a lot about which color would look best on each kitten. "The braided green one is for the little black kitten," Marion explained. "The bright purple satin collar is for the white kitten. The red velvet will look great

on the black and white kitten, and the pink collar will really stand out on the silver kitten. The sunny yellow collar goes on the dark gray kitten." *Whew!* Marion took a breath.

"Great colors!" said Liz. "What about the tabby kitten?"

The tabby kitten was the one with the healing paw. Marion was saving his collar for last. "I've got something extraspecial planned for Ollie," Marion said with a smile.

The name had been Marion's suggestion. All the girls gave Ollie extra care and cuddles, but Marion had a special place in her heart for him. His brothers and sisters could now run and jump and play. But poor Ollie was still limping around a little. He would often sit off to the side and watch the others.

Sometimes Marion felt like she and Ollie were going through the same thing.

Marion reached for her clipboard. She checked the list. "So what's left to do before Saturday?" she asked.

"Mom and I are baking another batch of cookies tonight," said Amy. "We've got six dozen so far! We're going to bring a big cooler of lemonade, too."

"Great!" said Marion, making a note on her list. "Food, check!"

"And I've got almost all of the

decorations ready," said Liz. "I'm
still making some really long
paper chains in bright
colors. We can hang
them all around the
sides of our table.
Tonight I'll make
the sign!"

"And Mom helped
me put new batteries
in my karaoke

machine," Ellie added. "Now I'm thinking up catchy things to say at the horse show. What do you think of this?" Ellie held an imaginary microphone to her mouth. *"Kittens and cookies! Cookies and kittens!"* she boomed.

The girls laughed at Ellie's announcer voice. "That will get people's attention, all right!" Amy said.

Marion checked things off on the list. "Decorations, check! Karaoke machine, check!"

There was one other thing Marion wondered about. "Guys, how will we know who *should* adopt a kitten—who would give them a good home?" Marion wanted to make sure the kittens would be taken care of.

"Good thinking, Marion," Amy said. "My mom will be there the whole time, so she can talk to people about having kittens as pets."

Marion nodded. She knew that

Dr. Purvis would make sure the kittens went to loving families.

She hated the idea of any of the kittens living somewhere they wouldn't be loved . . . especially little Ollie.

Kittens and Cookies

"Wow!" said Liz, leaning close to Marion. "There are a lot of people here!" She had to speak up. Right next to them Ellie was half talking, half singing into the karaoke machine microphone. She couldn't quite contain her musical side.

"Kittens and cookies! Come have a looksie!"

"Lots of people *and* lots of horses!" Marion replied to Liz.

The horse show was being held at the Santa Vista fairgrounds— near Ms. Sullivan's house. There were two big performance rings, and stands for people to sit and watch. The parking lot was full of cars and horse trailers.

The girls and their parents had come early. They had picked a shady spot, between the parking lot and the performance area, where they had set up the booth. It was made out of Marion's family's beach

The Critter Club Presents:
"Meet the Kittens!"

umbrella and Liz's family's big folding table. With Liz's decorations and sign, the girls thought it looked great!

The kittens were playing happily in a little fenced area behind the table. Ms. Sullivan had brought them over from The Critter Club.

Earlier Marion had put on their special new collars.

"They all look sooo cute!" Ellie squealed. "And I love Ollie's collar, Marion."

Marion liked it too. It was a sparkly silver ribbon with a heart charm on the front. The other girls

To OLLIE, LOVE ALWAYS, MARION.

couldn't see, but on the back of the charm was a message.

It had already been a busy morning! Lots of people were stopping by the booth. Some just stopped by for cookies and lemonade, but many others asked Dr. Purvis about adopting a kitten. Amy's mom was chatting nonstop!

Right before noon Marion took a

break. It was almost Gabby's turn in the ring! She went with her mom and dad to watch from the stands. It *was* hard to watch her sister ride, but not because she was jealous. She was nervous and *excited* for her little sister!

As Gabby did her routine, Marion was amazed—her sister was great! When Gabby finished, Marion cheered louder than anyone.

Back at The Critter Club booth,

Marion could hardly wait to tell her friends.

"She and her horse both looked so calm. Their walk, trot, canter, and gallop was the best I've seen them do!" Then Marion noticed that there were only three kittens in the little play area. "What happened to the black, the white, and the silver kittens?"

Dr. Purvis smiled. "Three of the families from this morning came back," she said. "They wanted to adopt. I'm sure they will give our little friends great homes!"

Marion smiled happily. Secretly, though, she was glad none of the families had chosen Ollie. She would have been sad to have missed saying good-bye.

The hours sped by. More people stopped by the booth. One by one the cookies disappeared and the lemonade cooler got emptier. Ellie's voice had gotten tired, too, and she had turned off the karaoke machine.

The Critter Club Presents,
Meet the Kittens!

Before Marion knew it, two more kittens had been adopted—Ollie was the only one left.

The horse show was almost done. The loudspeaker came on, and Marion could hear a voice reading a list of winners. *Last year they read my name,* she thought sadly. *Not this year.*

Just then Marion *did* hear her

name announced!

"The junior division blue ribbon goes to rider number fourteen, Ballard." That was Marion's last name! Then the announcer went on: "Congratulations to Gabby Ballard!"

Marion gasped and clapped. Her sister had won a blue ribbon!

Chapter 10

Surprise!

What a day! The girls had found homes for five kittens *and* Gabby had won!

"I'm so proud of you!" Marion said to her little sister. She gave Gabby a great big hug. At that moment seeing her sister win was even better than getting her own blue ribbon!

"Let's celebrate!" said Marion's mom. She invited all the girls, their parents, and Ms. Sullivan back to their house for dinner.

Together everyone packed up the booth. It took Marion's dad a few extra minutes to get the umbrella back in their car. Then Marion and Gabby and their parents were on their way home—with Ollie. He sat, all alone, in a cat carrier at Marion's feet.

"Don't worry, Ollie, we'll find you a home," she said to him.

The Ballards were the last to

467

arrive at their own house. Marion's dad and sister took Ollie inside. Marion's mom got the crutches from the trunk. She helped Marion out of the car and up the walk.

When Marion hopped through the front door, she couldn't believe her eyes. There were balloons everywhere! There was a big cake on the coffee table. A colorful banner hung over the fireplace.

"Surprise!" everyone shouted. There was Amy, Liz, Ellie, and their parents; Liz's big brother, Stewart; Ellie's little brother, Toby; Ellie's nana Gloria; Ms. Sullivan; and Rufus, too! They were all looking at Marion!

"A party . . . for *me*?" Marion asked in shock. "But Gabby is the one who won."

Marion's mom gave Gabby a squeeze. "Yes, but now it's a party for you *and* Gabby!" she said. "We're very proud of you *both*, Marion."

Marion's dad put an arm around

her shoulders. "We know nothing has been easy with the cast," he said. "Missing the horse show was really tough, but you made the best of it. You put your efforts into working hard for The Critter Club."

He looked around at the girls. "All of you did . . . and it really paid off."

Marion felt great. Actually, she felt better than great. She felt *proud*. She hadn't won anything or gotten a perfect grade. Instead, she knew she had done an important job. "Finding homes for five kittens in one day *is* pretty awesome!" she said happily.

"You can make that six," said Marion's mom. She was holding Ollie.

Marion's smile disappeared from her face. "Six?" she said. "Has . . . has Ollie been adopted too?" Marion prepared for the bad news.

"Yep!" her mom said. "He's been adopted by . . ."

"*Us!*" said Marion's dad and sister together.

Marion's eyes went wide. One of her crutches fell over. She almost lost her balance but didn't. "Do you mean it?" she cried. "Really? Really, *really*?"

Marion's mom and dad smiled. "We really mean it," her dad said. "But there's one other person who has to agree."

Marion looked around in surprise. "Who?" she asked.

Her parents glanced over at Dr. Purvis.

"I can't think of a better home for little Ollie," Dr. Purvis said with a smile.

As Marion sat down on the couch, her mother handed Ollie to her. The rest of the girls gathered around Marion and hugged her and the adorable kitten.

"As soon as my ankle is all better, we're going to have lots of adventures together, Ollie!" Marion told the kitten.

Ollie purred and nestled happily into Marion's lap.

Read on for a sneak peek at
the next Critter Club book:

#5

Amy Meets
Her Stepsister

Amy's mom grabbed a potholder. She lifted the pot lid. Amy took a sniff.

"Mmmm," Amy said. "That smells *so* good!"

Inside the pot was a big batch of their famous chicken noodle soup. They had made it together. "The perfect dinner for a cool night,"

Amy's mom said with a smile.

Amy giggled. "Mom, this batch will last us all year!" It *was* a lot of soup for just the two of them.

Amy set the table. She put out two napkins and two soup spoons. Meanwhile, Amy's mom ladled soup into bowls.

Just as they sat down to eat, the phone rang.

"Start without me!" said Amy's mom, popping up to answer it.

Amy slurped up some broth.

"Oh, hi, Eliot!" she heard her mom say into the phone.

Amy's face lit up. Eliot was her father. He lived in Orange Blossom, a bigger town near Santa Vista. Even though her parents were divorced, Amy got to see her dad a lot.

"Uh-huh," her mom was saying into the phone. "I bet she would love that!" She looked over at Amy and smiled. "Why don't you ask her?" Her mom held out the phone to Amy. "Your dad has a question for you," she said.

Amy jumped up and took the phone.

"Hi, Dad!" she said. "What's up?"

"Hey, kiddo," came her dad's voice through the phone. "How would you like to spend this weekend at my house?"

"Really?" said Amy. She loved her weekends with her dad. "But I thought that was *next* weekend."

"I know," her dad said. "But I've got some really big and exciting news to tell you."

News? "What is it?" Amy asked.

"You know what? I want to tell you in person," her dad said. "Oh! And Julia is going to come visit on Saturday too."

Julia was Amy's dad's girl-friend. He had met her about a year ago. Amy really liked Julia. She still kind of wished her mom and dad were married. But since *they* didn't want that, Amy was happy her dad had met someone as nice as Julia.

"So I'll pick you up tomorrow. Okay?" her dad said.

"Okay! Bye!" said Amy, and she hung up the phone. She was so glad she wouldn't have to wait too long for the weekend. After all, tomor-row was Friday!

Then it hit her. *Friday.* It was sleepover night with her three best friends: Marion, Ellie, and Liz. They had a sleepover almost every week.

With a pang of disappointment, Amy flopped down into her chair. "Oh no. This means I can't go to the sleepover at Marion's."

Amy's mom patted her on the back. "You'll have fun with your dad, sweetie. And when we host next week's sleepover, we can make it extraspecial."

Amy nodded. *Besides,* she thought,

we have lots of sleepovers. But how often does Dad have big, exciting news?

Now she was really curious. What *was* the big news?

A Lunchtime Mystery

Amy couldn't wait for school the next day. She wanted to tell her friends about her weekend with her dad—and the mystery news! Lunchtime was their first chance to talk.

"Maybe your dad is going to run for president!" Ellie said excitedly. Her brown eyes twinkled. "Or he is going to Hollywood to be in movies! Or he found out you're related to the Queen of England!"

Amy giggled. Ellie just loved the idea of being famous!

Marion slurped the last of her chocolate milk. "Maybe he will take you on a shopping spree!" she suggested.

Then Liz spoke up. "Maybe your dad wants to write about The Critter Club in his newspaper!"

Hmmm . . . , thought Amy. That was a possibility. Amy's dad was the editor of a newspaper called *The*

Coastal County Courier. He knew all about The Critter Club. It was the animal shelter that the girls ran in their friend Ms. Sullivan's barn.

"That could be it," said Amy. "My dad did say one time that it would make a good story—how the club got started."

And it actually *was* a good story. Before the four girls really knew Ms. Marge Sullivan, they had helped her find her missing puppy, Rufus. Then Ms. Sullivan had a great idea. She decided Santa Vista needed an animal shelter to help lost and stray animals. Ms. Sullivan had an empty barn, and the girls had a love of animals, and that's how it all began!

It helped that Amy's mom was a veterinarian. Dr. Purvis taught the girls how to take care of the different animals that had been at The Critter Club so far: bunnies, kittens, dogs—even a turtle and a tarantula!

"Well, I am sorry I won't be around this weekend," Amy said. "I wanted to help out with the eggs."

They were incubating a dozen

chicken eggs at The Critter Club. A local farmer had dropped them off a week before. His family had to move. They had sold or given away most of their farm animals. Then, before their move, their best hen had laid a clutch of eggs. But she didn't want to sit on them. Amy's mom said sometimes hens did that.

Luckily, the farmer knew about

The Critter Club. He had brought the eggs and the incubator. The girls were so excited to help them hatch. Then they would find the chicks new homes!

"Don't worry," said Liz. "We can handle the eggs. They're not due to hatch for another week."

"But we will miss you at the sleepover tonight!" Marion said. She put an arm around Amy's shoulders.

"Oooh! And call one of us when you get the good news!" Ellie begged. "I can't wait to hear it!"

Callie Barkley

loves animals. As a young girl, she
dreamed of getting a cat or dog of her
own until she discovered she was allergic
to most of them. It was around this time
that she realized the world was full of
all kinds of critters that could use some
love. She now lives with her husband and
two kids in Connecticut. They share their
home with exactly ten fish and a
very active ant farm.

Marsha Riti

is an illustrator based in Austin, Texas.
Her premiere picture book is
The Picky Little Witch. She likes to take
long walks, stopping frequently to pet
neighborhood kitties.

the CRittER club

Join the club!